Ashley C

TALES
OF
WOODLAND
& HARVEST

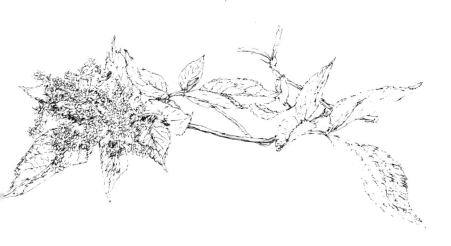

East Anglian Magazine Publishing Limited

By the same author:

THE LONG FURROW

THE KHYBER CONNECTION

HEART OF OUR HISTORY

Published 1990
Reprinted 1994

East Anglian Magazine Publishing Limited
Duke Street, Ipswich, IP3 0AJ

Printed in England
by Five Star Printing, Ipswich.

For
'Curly'
of Harvest Home

Who although a character of fiction, will still be known — by many different names — to countrymen the world over. To be more specific though, I dedicate this book to *all* the mechanics, fitters and storemen, without whom modern agriculture could not continue and particularly to all those who have helped me personally at —

Ernest Doe & Sons, *Sudbury*
Mann Egerton, *Ipswich*
Manns, *Saxham*
Blythe & Pawsey, *Ridgewell*
Cowies/Eastern Tractors, *Steeple Bumpstead*
Chaffers, *Mendlesham*

and
in especial memory of
John Risby
late workshop foreman at
Ernest Doe & Sons, Sudbury

A WORD OF THANKS...

... to Benjamin and Deborah for all their help, but most especially to my sister Jane for introducing me, many years ago, to an Australian called ... *'The Man From Snowy River'* ... who inspired my love of rural folklore.

The extracts from *Imagin*
by John Lennon on pages 35 and 37 are by permission of
BMG Music Publishing Limited.

CONTENTS

I

II

Part I
OLD FOOL

"That's 'keeper' Charlie Hurrell all over!" muttered Stanley Harris with a laugh. "He's such a miserable owd devil that no one ever could get on with him."

"Own worst enemy all of his life," agreed Hory on that long winter's evening in the Wenington *Bells*.

"Only time he ever talked to you was when he had something to complain about."

"That used to run in his family," said Horace. "I've heard different ones say that his father was as cantankerous as hell".

"Good job he never had no children!"

"Weren't no chance of that. No woman would have ever been soft enough to have him!"

It was a deserted Monday night pub. The hands of the big 'Railway Station' clock on the brown wall of the public bar suddenly jerked forward by another two minutes and pointed to a quarter past ten.

"Another one before you go?" suggested Horace.

"Make it a half, if you like."

The landlord, distracted from reading the racing page in the *Daily Mirror*, sombrely filled up their glasses, gave Horace his change and without a word returned to the stool from where he could watch both bars.

"Cheers" said Stanley.

After a moment Horace smiled. "I'll tell you a story about Charlie Hurrell".

"Go on then".

"Well, it must be over twenty years ago now. In fact it was the winter when we had all that blessed snow and anyone who lived up a sunken road like we did in the Kings Hall Cottages were pretty much cut off for a while.

"Anyway, in those days there were still eight of them 'housen' up the Three Mile Lane, but over the years Sanderson kept selling them off until come the finish there was only myself, Charlie Hurrell and Robert who were locally born people still living there.

"Course, it was just my luck to have Hurrell for a neighbour. Well, you know what a daft old codger he is. Mean as a blasted stone. Always scheming out how to save a few pennies on this and that, and generally scrapping about half the night to earn a few bob more. It was absolutely typical of the old dar'vil that when the electric first came he decided that he didn't want nothing to do with it. And it was just the same when 'young' Sanderson wanted to put us onto the mains water and sewerage.

"'He might want to put the rent up as well,' Hurrell had moaned, in his squeaky voice. 'And I remember the hard times even if you young'ns don't.'

"Anyway, come the finish, the rest of us had all got lovely houses with hot water and electric and proper Raeburns and damp-proofing installed. All except Hurrell, that is. The old fool. It was as if he enjoyed living in the past. I mean, you'd be going indoors on some cold, wet winter's afternoon, when he'd come struggling by with a wheelbarrow full of firewood that he'd pushed all the way home from Kings Wood and every two or three yards got stuck in the mud. And then at bedtime, you'd just about be getting what you might call 'cosy' with your missus when you'd suddenly hear him stumbling about next door with an old Tilly lamp and you'd say, 'Watch out, gal — do we shall all be on fire in a minute!'

"As for his garden — oh dear — you never saw anything like it. Talk about mad inventors! I mean, you had to respect him in a way. He was a rare old 'schemer', I'll give him that. But the devices he made up! Ought to have been in the Science Museum. He had it so he could lay in bed and pull a cord to frighten the sparrows off his garden first thing Sunday morning. Then he made a tin cat to patrol his lettuces. Well, that wan't cute enough for him. So off he goes and buys a lot of scrap curtain rail and builds a little track where this tin cat on wheels can run along. Come the finish, he even made a little windmill to pull it along the rails, out of some lead weights and balances that he's salvaged from an old grandfather clock.

"Anyway, that was Hurrell all over; and like I've said afore, he was someone whom you could have learned a lot from — and even admired in a way. I mean, he was a 'witted' old man — but he never wanted any friendship or company. And what you don't want in life, you don't get.

"Daft though, how he used to go to work with his wheel-barrow; leave it in Kings Wood during the day and load it up when he came home at night. Talk about work! I've never known a man to work like him! I'll give him that. I mean, he only had an axe to fell and split all this wood with. But no, you could never, ever, tire him.

"Worst of it, though, was that he would aggravate people so with his endless mutterings about having saved a few more coppers on the coal. Up in the village it got so bad that the young 'uns used to holler out, 'Whoa! Here come ol' miser Hurrell, the barrow-man'. Then they discovered that it was a rare old game to pinch his precious logs and then hide up and watch the old man stomp and storm about in a rage when he got home from work. He'd get as roiled as hell!

"His real problem, though, was that his whole life was just work, work, work. Come to think of it, by the time he'd got home at night and then lit his stove, got his Tilly going, carried up his water, chopped his firewood, cooked his grub and sorted out all the gadgets in his garden, it was a wonder he ever got time for sleep. And all the time we were living in comfort next door, with electric lighting, coal stoves and even central heating.

"Anyway, one Saturday afternoon about the middle of December, there was a 'hell and all' of a downpour so I was sheltering in my garden shed and talking to Robert. Course, who should come struggling along, grunting and coughing and wheezing and looking half drownded but old Charlie.

"'Silly old fool you are. You'd damn well kill yourself for two halfpennies,' called out Robert.

"'Ah,' he say, in his high pitched voice, as the water ran off his cap, 'we shall see. The pheasants aren't in the woods yet.'

"'What the hell are you on about, Hurrell?' I asked. But he only squinted, shook his head and went squelching along. 'Daft beggar,' I muttered, 'he will be the illness of hisself and we shall be forever biking up the village to telephone the doctor!'

"'Well, we shan't change him now,' grumbled Robert, with a sigh. 'I know by what my grandmother used to say.'

"'What was that?' I asked without a lot of interest.

"Robert looked at Hurrell who was tugging his barrow through a deep rut. 'She used to say that there's a lot of fools in the world...' he paused and yelled out so that Hurrell could hear him, 'BUT THERE AIN'T NO FOOL LIKE AN OLD FOOL!'

*   *   *

"But I've got to be honest and admit it. For Hurrell was right in a way. The weather *was* too hot for December. Oh no. it wasn't really any surprise when three days after Christmas the whole sky went a pale grey colour. Next morning there was six inches of snow on the ground. More to the point, there was a blizzard of a wind, about a force 10 from the east, I shouldn't wonder. Come dinner time, the ol' guv'nor growled, 'You shan't want the lorry for the next month now, Hory.' He was more than right. It lasted for seven weeks in total. It was February 21st before our lane was clear again.

"Of course, to begin with no-one minded much. But come the end of a month there was a real crisis on. The coal was getting mighty short — and there was no way we could get any more; the electric packed up and the water pipes burst and everyone got as miserable as sin.

"That's a curious fact of life, though. And I've got to give it to him straight. For during those seven weeks, old Charlie did soften up a bit. I mean, first he lent me and the missus an old Tilly lamp, then them next door borrowed his big water bucket

. . . The sunken lane . . .

when their pipes burst; and once the mains water packed up he did allow us — in a begrudging sort of way — to use the pump in his garden.

"The trouble was the snow hung about for so long. By the fifth Sunday we were *completely* out of coal and then the blessed power lines came down again and the kiddies' bedrooms went as cold as ice boxes. Worse still, the house at the end with the central heating got totally froze up because the Irishman, 'Sean O'Bill' as we called him, had used up all his heating oil.

"Anyway, that afternoon, things got so bad that the rest of us got together and had a little conference. As you can imagine, it didn't take us long to reach a decision. The Three Mile Lane was still full of snow and there was no other way that a vehicle could reach us. So, tails between our legs, we went up to Charlie to see if we could possibly buy some of his precious firewood. But, oh God! He is an awkward old cuss! The moment he saw us approaching, he went shuffling off into his cottage. Next thing was, he made out that he couldn't hear us knocking until we'd stood around getting cold for about quarter of an hour. Finally, he came wandering out, with a vile smile on his pokey ol' face and pretended to be deaf. Course, all this time we had to be as meek as hell whilst Sean tried to butter him up and said how very wise he was for putting so much firewood by — and was there any possible chance that he might be prepared to sell some of it? Oh, yes. We had to swallow humble pie that day, I can tell you. Old Charlie Hurrell made sure of that! Well, he kept up his game a little longer and then feigning surprise, declared, 'Oh, really! So you want to buy some of *my* firewood! Well, my, my!' And I stood there thinking, 'you vindictive old bugger!'

"However, he took me back a bit for the next moment he glanced up at that sullen white sky — perhaps whilst he was reckoning out how much he could charge — and then muttered cautiously, 'I don't see why not. That's going to set in a lot worse yet.'

"Well, Robert was shuffling about and I think he felt embarrassed as hell. 'Does that include me and Horace as well?' he asked. 'I mean, we've said some pretty harsh things on occasion.'

"'Provided you pay for it,' he declared, 'then it includes all of you.'

11

"I mumbled something about being grateful but the old man just bent over very slowly, picked up a short piece of wood, brushed the snow off it and without speaking, thrust it into Robert's hands. Then he pointed with his arm, in his stumpy sort of way, to the inky outline of Kings Wood. "'Here,' he said, pausing for a moment to pull his flat cap further over his forehead, 'I'll tell you suffen that'll size it up pretty well.'

"'Go on,' I said penitently.

"'Well, there are all sorts of fuels in this world . . .' and then he paused. And I honestly mean it, because I've never seen him try to crack a joke before or since — but the faintest trace of a smile came over his leathery old face, but then it faded and his voice became resentful again.

"'Yeah — there are all sorts of fuels in this world — but there ain't no fuel . . .', he paused again until we had both nodded in agreement, 'LIKE AN OLD FUEL!'"

HARVEST HOME

I suppose that this is one of the eight basic stories. Already some of you will have guessed, from the title alone, how it ends. Many of you on the Suffolk-Essex border will know the main character involved.

'Curly' Dawson. That's right. Him. Old Curly who worked for nearly fifty years at Mathews, the tractor and machinery merchants out along the Studbourne road. If you've been involved in farming in any way at all, then you must have met him. He certainly knew you. I shouldn't think there can be a farm between Cambridge and Colchester that he hasn't visited. I mean he'd been at it all his life joining Mathews the day he left school, just before his fourteenth birthday. You see, his father and grandfather were both blacksmiths at Nauston and I think that might have helped him to get the job. Course, when he started off, he was only the grease and lamp boy in the workshop but he had a gift for engineering and it wasn't many years before he was working on the petrol/paraffin Fordson tractors of the nineteen thirties.

Anyway, Curly made the job his own. Dozens of older people have told me how they remember seeing him last thing of a night-time, covered in grease and oil, scampering about and sorting out a broken down tractor — while a taciturn old farmer, more accustomed to horse-drawn implements, watched him with sceptical approval.

The thing was, he was *always* out and about. That's how he got to know so many people. Mending up binders at harvest time, replacing worn sprockets and bearings in the winter and always willing to service and tinker about with an early combine. By all accounts, he loved it. Even at the end of his life, his twinkling eye would light up as he described those frugal and pioneering times when agricultural mechanisation was in its infancy.

"When I first started," he used to laugh, "We had to bike out with our spanners and then go coit-ing around trying to find some old farm up an overgrown lane miles away from anywhere. Well, you'd done the better part of a day's work by the time you got there! Anyway, when you'd finally found the place, you'd have to change a head gasket or some such thing, and likely as not you'd be in an old tumbledown cart lodge that was half full of straw with an ol' sow or two grunting around you and a lot of ol' chickens scratching about and every time the old farmer came stumping out to growl and moan at you, his blessed dog would scarify all the hens about so that they'd be a nan-a-king and fluttering all around and there would be hell an' all of dust and chobs about! It's a blessed wonder them old tractors ever ran at all!"

Those were the halycon days of his life! When he — Curly — was a part of that extraordinary transformation which took farming from the horse age to the era of sophisticated tractors and modern combines. What a wonderful contact he was for a rural historian and how much I enjoyed interviewing him as he sat in his wheelchair and reminisced.

Ah yes. The wheelchair. Arthritis was the reason. In recent years it afflicted him terribly and finding repair work increasingly painful, he had volunteered to take on the storeman's job at Mathews' depot.

Often, during these more contemporary times, frustrated, irritable farmers, like the author — panic-stricken with a harvest breakdown — would come tearing in to Mathews' store for spare parts and seeing his square, firm face and happy eyes, would suddenly relax, the tension dissipated as they bellowed out *'HEL-LO, CURLY! Do you remember that old crawler that blew* up thirty years ago . . . well, we're STILL in the headest muddle out!' And when he had assembled the 'knife sections', the 'fingers' or the pulley belts that they needed and written out the myriad of part numbers (God knows how these storemen keep themselves clear-thinking!) the farmers would amble off, their impatience and anxiety eased away.

To tell the truth, it is only men like Curly who truly understand those of us still working on the land. How utterly dependent we are upon them.

That's why it is a shame we didn't get up a collection when he took his early retirement — after forty nine years of service — but now wickedly crippled with that awful disease. Several people did suggest the idea but no one person took a lead to organise the fund. It was left to Curly — out of his own meagre pension — to purchase the colour television and Citizens Band radio which were to bring him so much pleasure in his final months.

Well, I suppose this is one of the oldest stories of all time but it is also one that I have got to repeat. And if it reads rather crudely, it's because I'm writing it on our first Sunday after harvest and the last few weeks have reminded me again of that incident with Curly which occurred almost twelve months ago on the final day of harvest — Saturday September 10th — last year.

That was the harvest that Gordon Preachley from Studbourne, and Andrew Wing, the vicar's son from Castleton, were with us as summer students.

July and August had been notoriously wet and the whole campaign had been a long and arduous uphill struggle. Sometimes we managed to snatch a few hours combining before the sky went grey over Hestup to the West and we had to rush the trailers back towards the barns. Then, as the rain drove down in torrents, we scurried back to clear the trails of mud from off the Fulmer road and tried to find a sheltered spot to poke the mud out from the balmed-up 'concave' of the combine's threshing drum. Twice we had the trailers stuck axle deep in mud. And the hilliest land — which overlooks Wenington Church — with its 1 in 8 gradient — had to be combined all one way because the ground was just too soft to maintain traction on the uphill slopes. Even then the Claas slipped and slithered about sideways, picking up mud and stones along the bottom auger and breaking the 'lifters' off the cutter bar. Meanwhile, the ancient grain drier fairly hummed and glowed in a valiant attempt to clear the mounds of soggy grain which built up around the intake pit like hot and stodgy hillocks.

In early September — as so often happens after a wet August — the weather perked up and for a few days it was a case of 'Crack on!' and 'Go like hell!'. Joyfully, by six o'clock on the Saturday evening, only about two acres of wheat remained and I told Gordon and Andrew that they might as well go home.

Ten minutes later, the little crack in the main 'straw walker drive-belt' became a tear. Instantly the alarm hooters and warning lights were activated as straw jammed up in the back of the combine. Horrified, I slammed down the throttle and cut out the works; jumped down the steps and rushed to the rear of the machine, panic-stricken to find out what had gone wrong. Frantically opening the pressed metal guards, I took one look at the belt and swore with exasperation that fate should thwart me with so little left to do.

*　　*　　*

It was nearly eight o'clock by the time I had returned from Manns of Saxham with a new double 'V-belt'. The sky was quickly darkening and as I drove across the swishing stubble of the field I could only just discern the two tractors and trailers that Gordon and Andrew had brought out and left, parked in the right direction — facing downhill towards the gate.*

Furthur away, across two dusky fields, the lights of the massive Ford tractor with the six furrow plough blazed out at front and rear whilst beneath them the smoothly polished 'mouldboards' shone out like silver spears.

Meanwhile on the northern skyline — across by Horley Church — the flashing of an amber beacon signalled a waiting grain tank whilst on other fields a mass of bright flourescence, broken only by the rotations of the 'reel' told of other combines still at work . . . Like my neighbours I was also determined to finish that night.

* so you don't have to pull the load uphill on wet land.

16

Getting out of the pick-up, I opened my tool box and turned towards the combine. Looking at the sequence of drive shafts and pulleys, my heart sank. There was a guard to take off first, a hydraulic pipe to be disconnected, another belt to be removed and a shaft and bearing to be eased off.

Suddenly feeling very tired and beaten, my resolve began to weaken. It had been an exhausting season. I would have my tea first. Maybe the energy and motivation would come back later and I would set about the 'V-belt' then.

Clambering back into the cab I plucked my dinner bag from beneath the operators console where the warning lights glowed out with dappled colours in the darkness.

As usual I poured out the flask of tea and balanced the steaming plastic cup upon the gear change column — where it just fits — put my legs up to rest on the handle of the door, placed a tupperware box of cheese, peanuts, lettuce and tomato on my thigh and another with flapjack and honey sandwiches on the operator's console. On the khaki trousers of my other thigh I balanced the operator's manual and scrutinized the drawing of the drive shaft.

As I ate, a great and glowing moon of pale saffron rose over Fulmer Church and bathed the golden stubble of the fields in gentle yellow light. In the stillness of the night-time, an aura of the magical transforms those rolling hills and hollows from the worldliness of day into the tranquility of night. Beside me the line of poplar trees stood out as dark blue silhouettes — like sentinels of this secret dream land.

Sometimes the sensation is so enchanting, that spellbound, I almost ache from the wonderment of so much natural beauty. At that moment, also, one can almost see and hear the harvest gangs of old go by with scythe and flaggon, and visualise in turn the trundling wooden waggons with the heavy horses that waited for the pitched up sheaves and sense too, the conversation when the 'hobby rake' departed from the field and the gleaning gangs went in as children scampered round their mothers' ankles and then laughed and played and cried and sang. Children who are today within their eighth and ninth decade.

*   *   *

Returning to the present I glanced at the diagram of the drive shaft to be dismantled. Once again I felt the tiredness and shook my head. Then I heard some interference on the C.B., turned up the volume and checked my watch. It was almost half past eight. As had become customary during the past few evenings, I switched over to Channel 4. Some five miles away, in a small bungalow in Longford, an older, battered, arthritic-ridden man would be waiting in his wheelchair as he had waited all day long: in discomfort and disability, with one eye on his television and one ear to his radio.

Quite a few of us, when we were tractoring or at harvest, had made the effort to have a little chat on Channel 4. The voice that answered was always cheerful — God knows how — cracked the latest jokes, spoke about old times and generally laughed a lot and made us feel a good deal happier than before.

"Curly here!" a rumbustrious voice boomed across the ether.

"How are you?" I replied.

"Oh God, not you again, author boy! Well, what sort of a muddle are you in now?" he exclaimed with happy jest.

"Nothing at all!"

"Thought you'd be out with your mates being as it's Saturday night . . . " There was a pregnant pause before he continued in a voice which feigned surprise, " . . . Surely," he began as if astonished, "even *you* have finished harvest by *now?*" (Meaning, 'I bet he has had a breakdown!').

"I probably would have done if I didn't spend half the night talking to an old cripple like you!" I retorted with the healthy rudeness that is the bond and not the breaking of a male

18

friendship. "I've just been past your house on the way back from Mann's actually," I continued, (meaning, 'It would be quite handy to have old Curly stand by his C.B. for a while — I may need some advice').

"Daft beggar! What have you broken this time?" (I'd much rather keep talking to you than watch this 'ere junk on television!).

"Bloomin' old walker belt broke." (I wonder if he ever replaced one on this model of combine?)

"Ho! You've got a job on your hands!" (I discovered that on Brown's Farm six years ago.) "Anyway, I'm sure you can manage all right" (meaning, 'I'm pretty sure that he can't but I'm going to win this little game and make him ask me properly.")

"You've done one as well, have you, Curly?" I answered with cocksure bravado. ('Damn you.')

"Yes, I've changed several. Anyway, got to go now . . . the Two Ronnies are on T.V." ('I challenge you'.)

"Well, you can keep your C.B. on, can't you?" I responded quickly, with flagging self-confidence. (Actually, that's ten points up to Curly)

"Well . . . " he deliberately paused, " . . . I can do," he continued patronisingly, "If you think I can help you."

"I thought it might break the monotony for you a bit." (Five points to me).

"You know something?"

"What?"

"I reckon," he declared in a tone of mock exasperation and anger, "that you are just about more dumb than all the other farm boys I know put together!!" (Translation: 'but I like you and it's fun and it makes me forget the pain and the time goes quicker.')

"Suppose I must be to want to keep talking to you!" I replied with a triumphant laugh (meaning: 'I'd actually like to come and talk to you again about local history. And if I'm honest, it's only people like you who make me feel the farming job is still worthwhile').

"I'll call you back later, Curly."

"O.K. then. Over and out."

Smiling broadly and no longer feeling tired, I swung out of the

19

cab and jumped down the steps. Turning on the C.B. in the truck, I flicked across to Channel 4, picked up the new 'V' belt, switched on my big night-time torch, selected a range of metric spanners, a hammer and a screwdriver, balanced the torch on a recess, and set to work. The inner guard was held on by about eight 13mm bolts. It's incredibly frustrating to undo them all . . .

"I expect by now," came a voice as Channel 4 crackled into life, "that you've cut through the guard with your oxy-acetylene." ('You're impatient enough.')

"Course not, Curly. What do you think I am, bone idle or something?" (meaning: 'That's exactly what I'd thought of doing but now I won't, just to cheat you.')

"I should tie the 'hinged panel' back if I was you, then you won't catch your head on it . . . and lay a sheet or something on the ground in case you drop anything, otherwise you'll be half the night crawling about looking for a lost nut."

"Course I've tied the panel back," I answered truculently. (Actually I hadn't, until it swung round and trapped my fingers, but I should have done — it's an elementary first step). And yes: I had spread a canvas sheet beneath the combine. "You must think I'm a bit soft," I continued, wanting to get on.

"Oh well! I'm off to bed then," he replied.

"Hang about," I muttered, "there's a spring tightener on the pulley — how many turns does it need?"

"Tells you in the manual," he muttered curtly.

"I can't understand the damn thing."

"That's your bad luck."

" . . . Well, I didn't think you'd know anyway."

There was a long, long pause. Then came a voice with the faintest trance of superiority.

Got it done yet? Onto the next bit all right?"

"Oh, for God's sake Curly!"

I heard him laugh.

'Well, if I were you,' he said, 'I should give it five turns first. But is is a hell of a tight fit; whatever you do, don't slacken it too much. It's an absolute devil to get back if you lose all the tension. We had one at Hoston that took half a day to get right.'

Someone was trying to break into Channel 4.

"Sorry, breaker. This channel is 10-6, 10-6," I heard him say.

"I'll call you back when this nonsense is over," I cut in.

And so we carried on for another two hours of intermittent bantering and joking as slowly, stage by stage, he guided me through the dismantling of the pulleys, the hydraulic pipes and the dog-clutch to the removal of the bearing and the cross shaft.

"Just having a stretch, Curly," I called in at 10.15 (meaning: 'I don't know why the damn cross shaft won't come — I wonder how hard I dare hit it.')

"Suppose you've smashed the bearing up!" he replied, with a note of grim nonchalance but perfectly reading my mind.

"No, I haven't quite started hitting it yet." (In fact I had — but not very hard).

"Well, you've managed to get the 'key' out, have you?" ('Let's make sure that you're doing everything in the right order.')

"Yes. That wasn't too bad. It's the bearing and cross shaft that's worrying me," I answered.

"Sounds like slow progress." (meaning: 'the ol' boy's sounding tired. I bet he can't see too well, groping about in the dark with a torch and a 12 volt lead light.')

"You're right," I answered, the weariness surfacing again. "Look," I continued after a moment, "there's no other key or securing pin on the other side of the combine, is there?"

"No. Not if you've undone all the obvious things." ('I wish to hell I could be out there with him. I'd love it more than anything else in the world.') "I tell you what, though, there is a flange on the shaft mounting on the inside. It *should* be at the top but just occasionally they *can* work round. You could probably move it back with a narrow screwdriver. What I should do is this. Check both sides and then give it one firm tap with a 14lb hammer. Just *one* firm tap though and then call me back again."

"O.K. . . . . Cheers!" I muttered gratefully, dropping all the rigmarole and jargon.

*   *   *

Later, after the shaft was released and the new belt was slipped on over all the other pulleys (what a lot of work for one belt!), I brought a tractor and a trailer across from the headland and left it 'ticking over' with the headlights shining full upon the combine.

"You still there?" I heard him call on my return. I explained what I'd been doing.

"Thought perhaps you'd gone off after some woman," he bantered, laughing to himself. "Funny thing, though," he continued, "I've been thinking." Again he chuckled. "I did a job for your grandfather over in Suffolk once. That was a late night effort as well. It was on an old Case combine at the start of the Second World War. We didn't have to worry over much about the blackout though — it was as black as hell! And I should know! We were up half the night buggering about with a couple of old Tilly lamps that kept flickering and going out! That was a tidy game! Just typical of your lot! Funniest thing was this. They all kept saying, 'Must get on; must get on . . . one more good day and we shall finish harvest . . . ' Anyway, we just got it all mended when it started to rain like the absolute blazes. 'Must get on and finish harvest tomorrow!' they all kept saying. Huh! They didn't finish for another fortnight!"

I laughed, and as Curly continued, I tried to picture him in his wheelchair amongst the thick carpets and the soft cushions of his home, surrounded by the photos of his family. Beside him, his wife Emily, who had nursed him with so much patience, would be knitting and smiling warmly at his stories, despite having heard them all a hundred times before.

"Needless to say," he continued, "after the storm was over, I had to come biking home but, typical me, I had forgotten to bring my 'papers'. So old Grunty Johnson in the Home Guard who was posted at the Hall End crossroads got it into his head that he better make out to arrest me. Daft beggar! As if he hadn't known me long enough! Course, I hadn't got time to worry about his silly pranks and games so I just went biking off."

"'I'll shoot,' he yelled, 'I'll shoot!'"

"'Mind your toes, then,' I called back. Anyway he did shoot — just to scare me like — but actually right up into the trees above him. Well, of all the chanciest bad luck, he happened to hit a pigeon that was roosting there and, of course, just at the very moment that this 'ere pigeon came tumbling down, who do you think should come driving along on inspection duty? His C.O. — old Colonel _ _ _ _ _ _ _ ! It nearly landed on the Colonel's car, and Grunty got court martialled for 'gross neglect of duty'. Silly old sod! Served him right, that's what I say! Still, that's what you get for being hoity-toity and a cut above yourself!"

Feeling more relaxed, I laughed, picked up the spanners and then let Curly finish. "Anyway, that's how it was when I helped your grandfather — and that's a night I shall never forget!"

*   *   *

Apart from one awkward bracket, reassembling the remaining pulleys and tightening jockeys was a fairly straightforward job and I didn't need to seek Curly's advice again. Finally, just after eleven o'clock, I cleared away the tools and ran the combine for a couple of minutes to ensure that everything functioned smoothly. It worked! It was all O.K. and correctly aligned. Jubilantly I tried to contact Curly to thank him properly, but it was Emily who answered. "Curly has gone to bed" she began, — but next moment I heard him distantly bellow and laugh, "Must get on! Must get on! Worse than his ol' grandfather!"

And so it was that I finished harvest. A light breeze was blowing through the crop and the bright white heads of wheat were moving — swaying dry and husky in the headlights. It took only another forty minutes to complete those last two acres and by a quarter past twelve I had emptied the grain tanks, carefully idled and closed down the combine and taken the trailers to the off-hand barn. Harvest was over!

But what a night it was to finish. By now the enormous amber moon was ringed with gold and silver and crystal blue haloes and I could clearly see the outline of the hedges and trees some two or three fields distant.

Utterly exulted I strolled dreamily homewards as the crickets chirrupped from the grass beside the cartrack. Eventually I reached the farm buildings. Through the open doors of the long asbestos barn, the furnace of the grain drier cast flickery shadows across the concrete yard. Inside, the bright, khaki-gold wheat was rattling out of the augers onto a heaped-up pyramid.

Yawning profusely, I switched off the massive through-put fans. Their tone immediately changed, the propeller blades 'whirred' for half a minute and then, suddenly, the farm was quiet once more.

Harvest was over! We *had* made it! Thank God, there had been no injuries or accidents to anyone this year.

Closing the rattling barn doors, I thought again of Curly and wondered if I could remember even half of his humorous anecdotes of bygone rural life. I resolved to definitely interview him properly in the winter.

But at that precise moment, as I walked towards the farmhouse, what I felt was not historical interest but an overwhelming sense of triumphant pride. We had done it! Curly in his wheelchair, with all of his experience and knowledge, and me with the spanners — young, ambitious and too impetuous to think things out. But together we had succeeded! Curly and me. In the darkness and gloam of the night-time, we had finished the harvest of Hestup and Fulmer.

Opening the heavy farmhouse door, I wondered if any of my friends or relatives had phoned up that evening, or if there had been any private letters which would be waiting for me on the kitchen table.

But there were no messages and only a mundane assortment

of bills and adverts in the pile of mail. After a drink of hot chocolate, I soon went upstairs to bed.

But I shall never forget the next morning. For then there was a message. It will always be stamped in my mind. For I had awoken late and fumbled downstairs half asleep.

I opened the kitchen door. And saw it. Propped up beside my tea mug. The large brown envelope on which Mother had written the news. I glanced at it quickly. And my euphoria vanished.

I stood still. Stock still, stupified and disbelieving. I read it again, but the words didn't change. The meaning didn't alter.

"Neil Hawthorne from Mathews phoned early this morning . . ."

Utterly stunned, I sank into my chair.

The full details emerged later. In Mathews' store and then at the funeral. But at the moment, all I could do was try to accept. For the heart attack had occurred just after midnight and . . . and there was only one consolation.

Curly's harvest had been called safely home.

HAZEL

"A story about Hazel, eh! Who is she then, lover boy?" jibed my old mate, Pete Rawson.

It's exactly what he would say. And in a way he is right. This is a love story. But he's also wrong. For it's not of the love between human beings.

It's to do with a different love. And it goes back many years. Right back to the late sixties. 1967 in fact. And the love, and the story? You can smile if you like but . . . well — perhaps you'd better read on.

I was 15 in 1967. Strapping, strong and exulting in the joy of manhood first experienced. As for the farm? I loved it. In fact I couldn't work hard enough. Every minute of my summer holidays was spent at work — laying concrete, brushing out the barns, corn carting from the combine, and finally 'rolling' on an old grey 'Fergy' for interminable hours of jouncing and chankering across the leathery hard furrows of yellowy-brown clay.

But I also had another passion. Music. The music of the Cream and the Stones and Jimi Hendrix and most especially the Beatles, whose *Sergeant Pepper* had just been released, and which had raised John Lennon in my mind to the ultimate of heroes.

Not surprisingly, the minute I'd earned enough money, I went off to Studbourne and bought both the album and — a Philips Hi-Fi — as they were called in those halycon days when it really was a pioneering purchase!.

It was amazing. With the amplifier full on, I could hear it outside right up in Appleton Field by the old barn. But if I knew how to turn the volume up, I also forgot — like the teenager I was — when to turn it down, or for that matter, when I should go to bed.

On only the second night, I woke up my father and — er — it was just before midnight. Yelling crossly, he stormed into my room, swung round, and then tore down stairs to pull the trip handle on the fuse box and remove all the fuses.

Thereafter the same ritual was performed each night at 10.15 and I had to stumble around upstairs by torchlight . . . Oh to be a teenager again!

He was not alone in disliking my musical taste — or the ideas of my pop heroes. After all, this was the sixties. And the generation gap was maybe wider than any time before or since.

As always, it was the division between the solid and the fluid, the burdened and the free. Indeed, to my generation the Beatles and Rolling Stones were like the apostles of a personal liberty so different from the rigid strictures that had hitherto prevailed.

But to those who had so grimly survived the Somme and High Wood, the horrors of Dunkirk and D-Day, this limitless freedom was differently perceived. And as I helped to shovel up rye grass seed, the sturdy farm-workers with whom I worked ruefully bemoaned the passing of National Service and declared of my musical idols: 'Screaming pop stars! What they want is a damn good hair cut. A bit of army life would do them good!'.

I knew nothing then of limbs that ached with stiffness and rheumatics; of minds that carried tiredness forward week by week, and of that heavy, leaden weight of adult responsibility which crushes out the colour and frivolity from life itself.

Thankfully, though, the criticisms were always wryly made and likely as not amusing. Besides, in the evenings I could forget their reservations and the Philips would reverberate once more with, *All you need is Love, Purple Haze* and *Knights in White Satin.*

*   *   *

We finished harvest on September 5th that year and two days later I helped John Fulcher unload his massive D.7 caterpillar — with its rope-pulled 'donkey' engine — which we had hired for our bulldozing project.

Two tiny fields, so small as to be almost absurd for 'modern' farming, were going to be united. Granted it seemed a shame to remove the bit of hedgerow in the middle but somehow — at the time — it seemed inevitable.

Father drove the 'dozer. The caterpillar's old tracks rattled out noisily on the hard clay soil and could be heard across the valley in Lower Wenington. Meanwhile the rest of us, Old John and Derek, Hoppy, Bob and me worked the Ford 'Dexta' loader that pushed up the mounds of timber to be burnt, pulled out the lingering roots and rounded up the fires. For an easily impressed youngster, it was memorable work.

But as the men stopped for breakfast — hot tea and thick white sandwiches — they discussed the job with a typical balancing of opinions that remains a Suffolk characteristic.

"Blasted shame," muttered Derek.

"Times change," grunted Bob.

"I bet time 'e's paid all his expenses, it'll be twenty years or more before he gets his money back on this."

"That's the trouble with tractors," mused Hoppy slowly, "they make so many other changes necessary."

"Crying shame about the rabbit holes though," retorted Old John, nearing his retirement. "I got three good dinners out of this hedge last year, and we've picked hundredweights of black-berries . . . "

"Time we was children," said Derek, "we used to walk this way to school. Course, further on they were all meadows for horses that time of day."

"What do you think, Beatle," Hoppy suddenly asked me, with a mixture of hardness and avuncular condescension.

But before I could answer, Derek jibed, "Deaf, I shouldn't

wonder. The way he plays that gramophone of his. Sits right beside it. They say you can hear it up in Fulmer."

We all laughed but I was glad that I didn't have to say anything or take sides. Moreover I wasn't quite certain what I did believe. For a youngster it was simply fun to do an adult job.

It was Hoppy who spoke next, throwing the dregs from his flask into the crackling fire, and with everything that he said, I whole-heartedly agreed.

"Pity about the old lady in the corner", he sighed, pointing to a single tree some 200 yards away that stood on a little patch of grass beside an old, moss-covered stock gate which had not been used for thirty years.

In the distinct sunlight of that clear September morning, 'the old lady' spread out in a perfect symmetry like a parkland specimen, her graceful boughs serenely stretching skywards. Very, very slightly though did the trunk lean sideways — a few degrees from the upright — and yet curiously this gave the 'lady' an even greater sense of posture and a more perfect beauty in her own unequalled singularity.

"Shame to see her go," murmured John. "That's where my grandparents first met. Sheltering from a storm beneath that very tree. Grandmother was 'in service' up at the Hall and was walking home to Wickstead on her Sunday afternoon off. Grandad was a horseman at Hestup Hall . . . I heard 'em tell the tale a score of times."

"Did I ever tell you of the time we did an 'ambush' practice there with the Home Guard?" asked Derek, " . . . jumping out of the branches into a waggon-load of straw like a lot of clowns. Then some bright spark gave the horse a prod and it jerked forward just as old Grunty Johnson jumped off that big branch — the high one — and he missed the waggon and broke his foot. He was a-hobbling about for weeks on end with that!"

"Is it a hazel tree?" I asked.

Too late, I saw Derek and John wink at each other, the brown skin around their eyes crinkling into smiles.

"Good job we don't send you off for a bag of hazel nuts, boy," grunted John with friendly contempt. "He say, is it a hazel tree!"

"What the hell do they learn you at school if you can't tell the difference between a hazel and an elm?" chided Derek.

"It's over 200 yards," I began lamely.

"That is the trouble," cut in John, "all they've got in their heads nowadays is blasted old pop music and Beatle tunes."

I made the suggestion at tea time that we should leave the tree by Gallow Corner. Father thought I was mad.

"One tree in the middle of a field! You must be crazy! It'll be forever in the way! Whatever we do — combining, ploughing, drilling or beet harvesting. It'll be nothing but an infernal nuisance."

"Why couldn't we move the cart track?" I asked. 'Hazel' would be on the boundary then.

"Look," he replied, "everything's changed. We're living in a modern world now. A world of motorways and pylons, airports and power stations. But you mark my words, son. The bad times will come back for farming and only the efficient will survive."

I guess it was my fault really. If I'd had tact enough to let Dad think it was his idea, (the sort of deviousness that I've learnt with age) I might have got my own way. As it was — well, we are both as stubborn as hell — and agriculturally I suppose he was right. But as I left the room, frustrated and tense, I wondered if I had really done all that I could to save 'Hazel's' life.

That was the night when John Lennon appeared on television, with his squinting eyes and wire rimmed spectacles, and told us how the world was being destroyed by mankind's greed and avarice and hatred.

The only solution, he explained, was peace and simple living. At the time it was wonderfully easy to believe . . . it also seemed incredibly relevant! And so, later that night, my adolescent mind made up, I strode up the track once more, along North Field and towards the 'old lady'.

There was a brilliant harvest moon; and in the pockets of my overalls were four, American sized, spanners. What I had to do did not take long . . .

*　　*　　*

Next morning I returned to boarding school. The whole place was redolent with the smell of fresh paint and the interminable corridors reverberated with boisterous tales of imaginary exploits.

Fleming, my fellow 'second row' in the Colts rugby team, gave me a hand with the trunk.

"Jeez, man!" he exclaimed forty stairs up. "Are you carrying a dead body in here?" Yes, it was unusually heavy.

Next day I was summoned to the headmaster's office. In grave tones he ordered me to await my father at the main gates.

I suppose that to many readers the whole episode must seem unbelievably childish. But there and then we struck a deal. Father and son: in the first of many showdowns and manoeuvrings for domination.

I handed back the rope-pulled starting gear, complete with the nuts and bolts and the spanners. But 'Hazel' would remain, the cart-track would be moved and the upstairs electricity left on all night. In turn I undertook that there would never again be Beatles or Stones or music of any sort after ten thirty at night, and as a token apology I had to hand back my last week's wages.

*　　*　　*

The following summer I left school. However I still remained idealistic at heart and often thought back to my boyhood heroes and especially to Lennon, with his *Give Peace a Chance* and *Imagine.*

Hazel carried on as well. Aloof to all of the transient moods and fashions of mankind she continued year by year to perform her sacred ritual. And with each season that passed us by she yet revealed more grace and beauty and tranquil majesty than before.

Often, too, in those years, Hoppy or Bob would murmur about 'your 'ere Hazel'. For although the joke was long forgotten,

31

the nickname itself had stuck. When Hoppy drilled North Field, he would start by taking a line on 'the ol' boy's hazel tree'; and one year when he and Bob were chopping out sugar beet they told me that, "in two days time we should just about have got to your 'ere Hazel". At other times, also, when gleaning beet or inspecting crops and the sleet grey clouds with their sheets of icy rain sliced bitingly towards me from Hestup and Wickstead, I would rush across and shelter under Hazel's spreading boughs. Then, tight against her trunk, I would catch my breath and look across to Fulmer Church as the sky went dark and dull and the white poplars beside the path to Hogam Wood bent half a semi-circle backwards in the screaming of the Autumn gale.

Springtime and Autumn. Seedtime and Harvest; the eternal cycle that Hazel inscrutably witnessed until she, too, was caught up in the final act. And ironically, even in her passing, my teenage mentors were once again remembered.

In the end, of course, it wasn't THE Beatles that caused her sad demise. It was the other ones. The silver grey bastards: that measure a mere millimetre in length. The beetles that scientists call SCOLYTUS DESTRUCTOR and SCOLYTUS MULTIS-TRIATUS. Better known as Elm Bark beetles. The carriers of Dutch Elm disease. The disease which returned to Europe from North America in the late sixties as a mutated strain. A strain more virulent and deadly than ever before, to be borne from tree to tree upon these beetles.

The beauty and form of the English countryside was ravaged anew by Dutch Elm disease. It carried on where the bull-dozers and earthmovers left off. When the mind of commercial man said, "Enough!", Dutch Elm disease burst out in heinous destruction and said, "More, and more! and more!"

At Mound Farm it has denuded over two long miles of hedgerow and copse along. Before it, we had enough — just enough woodland to see the farm as beautiful and wooded — after it, the spinneys and the windbreaks that were such vital landscape features were obliterated and killed. It was a landscape disaster of the worst magnitude. It was relentless and without remorse.

For the next half century no newcomer will ever truly comprehend the extent of what it did. But it crucified the remnants of our countryside.

For a few more years, possibly because of her isolated position, Hazel survived unmolested. Majestically she lingered on, gracious and lovely, as the new plague — 'The Brown Death' — swept and swirled all around her, silently murdering every other elm on the farm.

Pitifully, we all hoped that maybe, just maybe, Hazel would be spared. "Perhaps a hard winter will kill off the beetles," suggested Hoppy one November afternoon ..." "Maybe the 'old lady's' become resistant to it ... " wondered Bob on another morning. And unashamedly we all prayed that on clear Spring mornings we could quietly rejoice and say: "The old lady has come into leaf once more".

Of course it was idle thinking. For nature has no remorse or conscience of any kind.

We first noticed the sickening tell-tale symptoms in 1977. There were little brown patches on the very crown of the tree where the leaves appeared to have had a premature Autumn — almost as if they had been scorched by fire. The following year it was worse. By early September whole boughs were leafless and the bark was shedding off like a scurvy skin. When the bark fell — from the highest branches first — we could see the signs of tunnelling that the scolytus multistriatus make as they seek their sanctuary and unwittingly transmit the fatal pathogen.

For a couple of years we left Hazel unfelled and still standing. Her great boughs and sweeping branches still formed a shape of perfect beauty that could suffer for a while the absence of their leaves. Even in death and as a skeleton, the loveliness of her fuller self lived on.

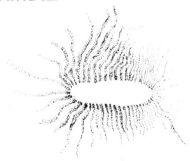

When the bark fell . . . we could see the signs of tunnelling . . .

It was a damp, misty December day when we finally cut the 'lady' down. It was one of those gloomy, lightless mornings when little specks of water form on your working clothes and the world itself seems half submerged in a Nordic darkness.

We went up the muddy, rain filled cart track on a Ford 6000 tractor, the spongy tyres squelching out the dirty puddles. On the back of the tractor was the black 'dump box' with the chain saw, the rips and the worn up tyres and cans of waste oil that we would use to make the fire.

"Rather be ill in bed than have to do this job. Crying shame, isn't it!" muttered Bob for us all.

We did all the things that you should do: cut a wedge into one side of the tree and then felled the 'old lady' safely onto Ley Field.

Next we built a fire to burn up the branches and the kindling twigs and bark. Every hour Bob crouched beside the glowing ashes — the right way for the wind — and sharpened up the chainsaw with three deft runs of the file per tooth. Later, we sliced through all the lighter boughs and carried them off the soggy field, making little sucking tracks and scattering the piles of sawdust where we trudged. Around us the tangy fragrance of the blue-white wood smoke blended in with the sweet aroma of the chopped-up branches as they oozed their sticky tar. Finally, as evening closed in, we cut through the main trunk twice and dragged it off the field onto that little grassy knoll where years before the old stock gate had stood.

We were all depressed as we hauled the final half-trunk off the field. For man and science and chemistry had failed us. Despite the moon trips and the nuclear power, the laboratories and the research specialists, the 'old lady' — like twenty million more before — had been taken from us. As with a pestilence of old, we were reminded of the frailty of man.

*   *   *

The mist and darkness swirled in early on that December evening. Bob and Hoppy 'knocked off' at five o'clock and took the other tractor to the farmyard. Remaining behind, I gazed sadly at the glowing embers of the fire and the silver ashes of Hazel's slow cremation. Then, a mile deep in thought, I walked across to Lenkins Field to switch off a banger on the oilseed rape before turning round and plodding back. Even in the dusky fog, the landscape was different and in the darkness my eyes kept seeking something that was no longer to be seen.

One always seems to work more slowly when alone. By the time I had rounded up the fire and packed away the chain saw and gathered up the fire for a second time, it was fast approaching six o'clock. In the flickering light, I glanced at my watch, anxious to catch the radio weather forecast so that I could plan out the next day's work. Getting into the tractor I turned the ignition key, stretched up to the radio and stabbed the left hand button for Radio Four.

It was music. Damn it! I must have pressed the wrong button. Again I looked up at the cab roof in the half light. I pressed the long wave button again. I *had* got it right.

It was still music.

And then I stopped.

For it was that very, very special music. The anthem which had become a hymn of hope − a psalm of pure idealism − for the generation of the nineteen sixties.

It starts with a piano, a simple acoustic piano. It is amplified seconds later until the notes repeat themselves and move slowly into melody.

And then, from across the ether came a voice − almost hoarse, slightly straining, as if the singer was finding it difficult to reach the notes of the words that he had written. I was spellbound. For even now the simplicity of the song creates a magic and an aura of its own.

> *"Imagine there's no heaven . . .*
> *It's easy if you try . . . "*

I leant back and for just a few seconds gazed out through the perspex window of the tractor's cab as the music flowed on.

The red embers of the fire glowed dully in the night-time and I thought fleetingly of Old John and Derek now laid to rest in the mossy country churchyards of Wenington and Wickstead with their own forebears around them. And with a special pang I remembered Old John. For never again would a strapping lad meet a blushing girl beneath Hazel's canopy of branches as his grandparents had.

And then the contemplations became my own. For I thought

'... Hazel'

also of the unmarked passing of one's life and time. And in that instant I recalled it all. Those years of simple altruism and of youthful expectation. That summer of teenage hope and of that momentous family showdown.

Now, beneath my very eyes, Hazel was fading and slipping away like the last portion of a candle stub as it flickers into the shadows of night-time.

Suddenly a stronger sob of the December wind aroused me back to the music.

"Imagine there's no possessions," the hoarse voice continued,

"I wonder if you can.
No need for grief or hunger,
A brotherhood of man.
Imagine all the people,
Cheering all the world.
You may say that I'm a dreamer,
But I'm not the only one,
I hope some day you'll join us,
And the world will be as one."

The staid voice of the Radio Four newsreader spoke over the final words as the music faded out.

"In memory," he said, "of John Lennon . . . who was murdered in New York, . . . earlier today."

"More than 20,000,000 elms were destroyed by Dutch Elm Disease which arrived in Britain in a cargo of logs from Canada in the 1960's". *The Times* 12.10.1987.

JOHN MACNAB

New Years Day! Two o'clock on the afternoon of January 1st. The sunshine sparkled on the frost of field and hedge, the heavens were a sky of cloudless blue; and on the far horizon, there hovered just a tint of rouge in the unfurling of an ember-glowing sunset, with an early moon and stars to glisten in the evening. What a day! And yet we were slumped in *The Bells*, with dull lethargic hangovers. Henry, Redhead and me. Unshaven and barely out of bed. Dumbly we sipped a beer after swallowing six or seven tar-black coffees. Guiltily we had all commented on the weather; and each of us was ridden with frustration that such a glorious day had been so totally mispent because of our indulgence the night before. What fools we were!

It was Daniel D'Lyster, grey haired, botanical and bookish, who perceived our plight and made the suggestion. He procures a living from studying the countryside and painting pictures of wild flowers. Overhearing us, he turned, and looking not unlike a classical tutor of old with his goatee and eagle eyes, augustly declared:

"I think you should do a John Macnab."

"Do what Dan?" mumbled Henry.

"A John Macnab!" he answered with a note of asperity, as if the name should have been familiar to us from the cradle. "I mean, if you really do want to be motivated on January 1st, then why not take out a poaching bet for next New Year's Day?"

"A poaching bet," murmured Redhead, as if the idea contradicted his most basic of morals. "Who was this John Macnab?"

"The hero of a John Buchan novel."

"Yes; but who was he?"

D'Lyster sucked on his pipe before answering.

"In legend," he finally began, "John Macnab was a gentleman of some means, who being bored with life, offered challenges to landowners that on a specified day, he would poach from their estate, a deer, a brace of pheasants, a salmon or whatever the estate was famed for. Now, being a man of honour, he didn't keep the booty for himself but actually delivered it to the landowner's house. However, if he wasn't able to obtain his bag – or was apprehended during his 'poach', he promised to pay the landowner a fifty guinea forfeit . . . or donate the money to a local charity."

"You are *not* suggesting that we follow suit!" said Redhead, with just a spark of enthusiasm in his otherwise exhausted voice.

"N-oo," replied Daniel coyly, "all I am telling you, is of a legend that developed long ago in Scotland."

"So it's got nothing to do with us then," declared Henry.

"It's only that in Buchan's novel, the character of John Macnab was actually a 'nom de plume' for three men . . . who just like you three . . . were jolly well in need of a little rejuvenation!"

"It would be impossible nowadays," murmured Henry.

"Besides illegal," said Redhead.

"And difficult to organise," I offered.

"Well . . . " began Daniel, with a provocative tone, "if you three aren't up to it . . . "

"We didn't say that," I replied. "We just said it would be difficult to do in practice."

"You mean you might fail because you are not skilful enough."

"Not at all!" I exclaimed.

"The point is," said Redhead, "it's against the law".

"So is after hours drinking!" quipped Daniel, as we all looked from our empty glasses to the big clock that hangs near the dart board. "No, I think that your principal objection is simply fear of getting up so early on New Year's morning."

"Rubbish!" cried Redhead, " . . . but . . . " he added after a moments reflection " . . . it would be *very* difficult in daylight."

"No" argued Henry, "It would have to be at night. I'd say it would be impossible during daylight hours."

"Not for three together!" retorted Daniel. "One of you could be a decoy, one could be a beater and the third could trap or shoot the quarry."

"Still sounds a tall order," repeated Henry.

"Well naturally: you would have to use some stealth. Maybe learn a few old fashioned tricks. Create a diversion. Get a decoy to lead the landowner's team away from you." D'Lyster halted for a single moment and then looking at me, added imperiously, "You like jogging! You could scuttle about and distract attention from the scene of action." The others smiled.

"Where would it be?" I responded, thinking of the terrain and wondering what I might have to do.

There was an immediate silence. Daniel I think, then allowed us to make a number of futile suggestions so that when he finally mentioned the obvious farmer, we were more ready to acquiesce.

*　　*　　*

"What about Ian Knightley of Kings Hall?" he eventually asked.

There was a silence. "He'd be ideal" I finally replied.

Despite this statement — to which the others generally concurred — there were still some reservations. Henry argued that he was just too nice; Daniel insisted that he would love it. Redhead believed that it wouldn't be feasible — his medium sized farm wasn't big enough; Daniel pronounced the odds to be dead even. I questioned whether it wouldn't be too apparent to Ian Knightley as to who this 'John Macnab' might actually be; Dan replied that discretion was up to us. Henry wondered how Ian's gamekeeper and son Justin, might react.

"They would be in their element," our mentor enthused.

"Who would compose and write the letter?" I asked.

"You," all three of them declared.

"Who's going to buy the next round?" I retaliated.

"D'Lyster!" we all retorted.

As we sat there in *The Bells*, — sometime I imagine after formal closing time — the sky began to darken to the East and the glory of the sunset refracted out across the Wenington Valley in the West and Daniel — persuasive as he is — padded up and talked his way with just a little laugh and hint of deferential courtesy, into yet another round, buying as he did, one also for the landlord. He also bought a Guiness for the ancient veteran who, for twenty years — and quite four landlords past — had sat beside the fire each dinner time and made a half pint last for however long it took for someone else to take the hint and 'fill it up again'.

His name at birth was Timothy James Hurrell. For one of those curious reasons, long since forgotten within rural lore, he had been, from that very moment, better known as 'Charlie'.

Every day to the minute at One o'clock, Charlie, now at least in his eightieth year, bicycled down from his flint walled cottage, past the pond which stands beside the Post Office, over the crossroads and on to the forecourt of *The Bells*. Having entered the village's single public house and proffered a customary greeting of "Same as usual, Landlord," he proceeded to his honorary seat beside the fire. Once ensconsed, he would listen to a great deal; observe all that went on; and say but very little. Now and then he would rock slightly forwards and spit noisily into the embers. Occasionally, through the gaps in his teeth, he would laugh at the misfortunes of his fellow man; grin when Henry (who was almost as regular) produced yet another new girl friend; smile at the memories of his younger days and sneer at the antics of the jumped-up rich.

"Of course Charlie!" exclaimed Daniel, as he passed him his stout. "You were involved in keepering on Kings Hall years ago, weren't you"

"That's right," came the reply. Hurrell was a man of little outward humour or warmth.

Over the years we had all been meticulously informed of his story. His father, genuinely christened and known as Charlie, had been the keeper for Sanderson at the Hall in the halcyon Edwardian era, when a bag of 200-300 had not been unusual. In those days, the estate still spread across most of the village and extended to over 2000 acres of rolling countryside: All of the land had been properly farmed by a variety of tenants although sporting pleasure had still been the landowner's greatest return on the capital invested.

Young 'Charlie' could just remember the tail end of that epoch. He could also remember — and quickly learnt — that gamekeepers trod a precarious path, being seldom much loved by the 'working man', and at best only patronised by the gentry. Worse, with the great depression of the nineteen thirties, the estate itself and all those whom it supported, fell on equally hard times. For years on end, neither Endings nor Hilltop nor Six Oak Farm, had either tenants or farmers; the land went derelict and the little army of housemaids and cooks; butlers and gardeners; carpenters and gamekeepers, once employed by the 'Big House', were slowly whittled away. By the time that 'old' Colonel Sanderson died, the Hall was hardly lived in, and young Charlie alone was keeper and gardener and woodman combined. In spite of everything however, he had continued with his father's great work, and year after year, his most dedicated hours were spent in the woods and the copses with his release pens and vermin traps.

Despite the more prosperous years after the Second World War, the Sanderson estate — like so many others — had received a body blow from which it never fully recovered and bit by bit, was eroded away. Hilltop and Endings Farm went to pay off the death duty on the 'old' Colonel himself. A row of cottages, Oaklane Wood and the Rookery smallholding, were auctioned to amortize the same tax when Marcus Sanderson was mortally wounded at the head of his platoon on a sand swept dune not far from Benghazi. Truemans Farm was similarly sold when an old tenant died and a sister had asked for her payout. And so it had gone on, like water slowly trickling from a dam, over thirty five years, until ultimately when 'young' Sanderson died in '72, the hammer came down and the remnants were finally disposed of.

Throughout it all, Charlie had lingered on at Kings Hall, now a mere shadow of its former self with just the 298 acres of 'Home Farm' around it.

Initially, the family of London financiers – the Voygels, who had purchased the Sanderson home, toyed with the idea of being modern day squires, resurrecting the shoot and then inviting their friends down from the 'city'. With this in mind, Charlie had been kept on. As inscrutable and taciturn as ever, he had continued to trap and to rear; to mow the lawns, brush up the leaves and to dig the garden and clear out the gutters.

Almost immediately however, the relationship between the Voygels and Hurrell became one that lost no love. "How the hell can I organise a shoot on 298 acres? They ought to rent the rights on the other old farms," Charlie incessantly grumbled.

For a while, Voygel had grimly tolerated the obstreperous old keeper. Friends of the Sandersons would patronisingly laugh and explain, "Old Charlie? Yes! Extraordinarily skilful, you know. One of the old sort. But an absolute law unto himself."

* * *

No-one ever did know, whether the accusation that Voygel made, "that Hurrell was out 'pinching and poaching' half the time when he claimed to be so hard at work," had any basis of truth or not. The Hurrells were independent and solitary people; They would always 'see that the gov'nor was all right' – but equally they weren't going to starve in the process. In point of fact, the details of the case on that dusky November night, were not particularly important. It was the outcome which was so crucially significant. For Hurrell and Voygel had an almighty great row. Hurrell vowed that he would never return to Kings Hall 'without honour' and Voygel, after furiously slamming his Range Rover door, watched the old man bike silently and bitterly away. Then, breaking into a gloating smile, he truimphantly drove back to Kings Hall.

Three years later, in June 1978, land values began one of their periodic escalations and Voygel unemotionally placed Kings Hall in the hands of *Savills,* the estate agents. After only two weeks of being advertised in *'Country Life'* and *'Farmers Weekly',* it was immediately sold to its present proprietor, semi-retired part-time farmer and shooting enthusiast, Ian Knightley.

The new owner with the courtesy and manners of a Jane Austen figure, heard of the tale of the old keeper and kindly suggested that he might like to 'do a bit now and then' on his old haunts once more.

Most of the old man's contemporaries thought that Hurrell was 'just plain stupid' when he refused. Sadly the old man appeared unable to differentiate between Voygel and Knightley.

Actually, the old keeper was ill. But it was no virus or physical condition that ailed him. Rather he was ill in the head. Ill with a fixation of the wrongs that had been committed against him; of the invidious insult that had been received; and the lack of any gratitude at all from Voygel or his sons. Worse, his fogged-up brain continued to reason that if Knightley had purchased Voygel's farm then he had also acquired the 'bad will' and the 'curse of the insult' that went along with it.

In time, Hurrell's preoccupation — of vindictively disparaging everything and everybody who was associated with Kings Hall — became a by-word for bloody-mindedness in the area. In fact, he was like a man with arthritic limbs whose movements are severely restricted. For Hurrell's ability — his mental elasticity — to forgive and forget had similarly siezed up and withered.

And so we sat there. With old Charlie Hurrell by the fire, whilst Henry and Redhead, Daniel and I, clustered together and busily discussed our 'sponsored poach'. And what a conversation it was! And how the ideas flowed. Oh yes! We schemed and drew maps and made plans. We analysed where the birds would be and which way they might fly, we discussed stalking and camouflage and how to finally deliver the booty without being detected or stopped. It was all heady, sporting talk.

Finally, the landlord hinted that it would 'soon be opening time again', and we began to depart. As we manoeuvred past the old keeper, he muttered with a sneer; "John Macnab: So that's who you are!"

"You'd better keep our secret!" declared Redhead.

"I'll keep your stupid secret," growled Hurrell. Then he wheezed deliberately and spat in the fire.

Eleven months passed, and the subject was quietly forgotten. But then, early in December, Daniel, Henry, Redhead and myself, found ourselves attending the same jostling Sunday drinks party. Amidst the clamorous repartee, someone raised the subject of New Year's Eve. A few minutes later I noticed that Daniel had discreetly disappeared. Half an hour later he returned. There was a mischievous twinkle in his eye.

He had just 'borrowed' our host's study, typed the letter from the "3 Macnabs" and posted it in a nearby letterbox. It was addressed to Ian Knightley. Five days later an S.A.E. arrived at the address of an anonymous friend in London.

The challenge had been accepted: D'Lyster had snookered us all.

From that moment the planning commenced in earnest. We obtained the largest map of the area that existed. We increased the scale and made it 50 inches to the mile. Then Henry and I marked on every area of potential 'cover' — be it a mature wood, a blackthorn thicket, a straggling hedge or a corner of kale or artichokes. Similarly, Redhead coloured in each field to indicate its cropping — green for winter cereals; brown for plough; yellow for oil seed rape and orange for the stubbles where we might most likely find our partridge. Next we thickened the North - South axis and then cut out some cardboard 'arrows' to indicate a variety of wind directions as we pondered where the pheasants and partridges were most likely to be found under differing weather conditions.

Later, black pins were placed on the map to indicate where the Knightley team could most easily survey us whilst red stars marked the likely locations of their poachers trip-wires and infra-red surveillance beams.

Finally, at the conclusion of that heady, protracted, meeting — which lasted until nearly 3 a.m. — we each placed £50 into an envelope. The letter was addressed to the Rev. C. Niven, rector of Little Wenington. A stamped envelope was also included on which I had typed the following address:

"Ian Knightley Esq.,
Kings Hall Farm,
Little Wenington."

We didn't provide our names, but simply requested the vicar to put the donation towards the Church Restoration Fund and to send a receipt to that excellent sportsman whose name was inscribed upon the S.A.E.

As the time drew closer, there were a multitude of finer points to clarify: Could we successfully use an air rifle? Where could we borrow an entirely anonymous vehicle? Did we each have a set of binoculars?

Within all the preparation our plan evolved. It relied on split second timings; the use of three walkie-talkies; Redhead's golden retriever; a couple of dummy pheasants; some fired cartridges; three whistles and a bag of pheasant feathers. In addition we would need an air rifle; a genuine 2.2; and a number of firework bangers.

*   *   *

Climatically, New Year's Day was in no way similar to the year before and a cheerless misty drizzle replaced the darkness of night-time. Nevertheless, as we struggled out of bed — with splitting 'party' headaches — to drink a few black coffees and consume a plate of eggs and bacon, an air of keen excitement soon possessed us.

By 7.15 we were ready for a final perusal of the 50 inch map, and adopted 'Plan B/3' (wind conditions still; no frost; overcast sky and damp.) Then, leaving Redhead's cottage, we began the quiet tramp alongside hedge and spinney until we joined the green lane — now overgrown and squelchingly bepuddled — that leads to Kings Hall Wood. Our hike, it seems, was a tactical success since Knightley's team were out patrolling all the nearby roads.

As we moved, I noticed Henry's countenance slowly change; that which for months on end had hinted at apathy was now incisive and alert to the quick; that which had been a touch of overweight was somehow lean and agile, and that which had appeared as the permanent lines of facial tiredness was youthful and supple anew. In front of him Redhead moved noiselessly, seeming to sniff the air with an ancient skill and his eyes — once glazed and bloodshot — were now restless, and observed the slightest detail. This was a Redhead I had never seen. A man returned to his natural element. Alive and alert in all his senses.

At 'Meadows Halt' we took a final reconnoitre. There was

no chance that pheasants would be spread out in distant hedgerows on such a day as this; nor was there any likelihood that cock birds would be squatting on the chilly winter barley stubbles. Unless the sun were to break through the enveloping quilt of mist, our struggle would be contained indeed — limited only to the covers on the edge of the fields; restricted to the woodland in the lower bottoms and centred on the osier beds beside the stream. For stealth and security it suited our purpose admirably. The brace of pheasants and the rabbit should present no problem. But of the partridge and the hare, we were less certain of our success.

At the Bottom Stile we checked our watches; switched on the hand-held C.B's; (arranging to move up 3 channels every hour); and finally separated to go our different ways: Henry in the leeway of Slade hedge to creep up to the maize and canary grass on Silent Hill; I, to take an almost opposite direction across to Kings Hall house and Redhead to crawl along the steep bank to the bottom of 40 Acres Field. Here, the great dark blackthorns straggled out like ancient stock-proof barricades, whilst beneath them, the bare soil was too shaded for even weeds to grow. It was to this that Redhead silently skuttled. Once there, he set up his snares, crawling along the prickly ground with leather 'thatchers' pads' strapped over his knees until, with half a dozen wires implanted on the slope, he worked his way to the top and set another ten amongst the sear and tufted grass where the runs were easier to discern.
discern.

Henry called us up at 10.15. We were then on channel 4. "Action," he muttered; "Do you both read and understand me?"

Fine and out we both agreed.

The minutes passed tediously. I imagined Redhead slowly moving through the damp maize and artichokes, his golden retriever leashed in until the final moment. Then I heard his voice again. He spoke one single word: "Excalibur!"

From the corner of the garden hedge, I leapt up and fired the starting pistol, lit the fuse rope on the pigeon scarers, fired two more blasts and clumsily ran along the edge of the rape field in full view of the farmyard and other vantage places of the Knightleys.

The mud along the cart-track bogged my feet down. In

plimsoles, the running might have been lightly accomplished. But in Wellington boots it was an excruciating task and I felt that every panted pace would tear my lungs out with exertion.

Approaching me from behind, I heard a Land Rover accelerating as it churned along the puggy track and from within it an excited shout. To the south I saw a tractor lurching recklessly towards my goal. But as I fired another blank, I heard two other fainter shots across on Silent Hill. I cheered aloud. My endeavours were not in vain!

Reaching the damp, ivy clad wall of the old kitchen garden, I hauled myself over — clutched quickly at the dummy pheasant that I nearly misplaced — glanced frantically at the faces in the approaching Land Rover and scurried through the opaque fog of the unpruned orchard towards the abandoned stables of Kings Hall. Weaving an erratic pattern, I found sanctuary at last in the loft of the tumbledown thatch barn. I was only just in time, for seconds later I heard a clamour of voices as my pursuers searched the orchard and the scotch pine wind-break. Without difficulty I recognised Justin Knightley, his girlfriend Susan and his father; Also Len, a neighbouring enthusiast and Michael and Jerry, two ever willing 'beaters' from neighbouring farms. Justin paused for a moment, entered the open portal of the dilapidated building, and in a fleeting glance missed the tell-tale mud upon the wooden wall where I had pulled myself into the loft.

"We've lost him," he yelled.

Moments later I heard Michael and Jerry being detailed off to take the Land Rover and patrol the further fields once more ...

It had been difficult not to pant; but now with the crisis over, I gulped in huge lung-fulls of foggy air and rubbed the sore muscles of my legs.

However, I was worried about getting cold — and seizing up — and of being spotted when I left the derelict building, for according to our rules, we only had to be touched by any of our opponents to exclude us from the game. I put my ear close to a chink in the wall, straining for any sight or sound that the orchard was still under surveillance. In the distance I heard a Land Rover and tractor reconnoitring towards the Silent Hill; in the farmyard I could just detect the excited mumble of a 'council of war' between Ian Knightley, Len and Justin. Seconds later they scurried off in different directions.

I glanced at my watch. It read 10.53. I pressed the C.B. close to my ear and quietly drew my jacket tight around me for greater warmth. At the pre-arranged time of 10.55 I heard Henry's elated voice. "Mission one completed and collected," (meaning: Redhead's dog had put out a hen and a cock; Henry had bagged them and the birds had been retrieved.) "Do you copy, No.3?" he continued.

"In hiding," I muttered. "Need half an hour to escape. Watch out your positions may soon be detected. The enemy are moving towards you."

Remembering to move up to Channel 7, I switched off the transmitter. Our conferences were to be held at 25 minute intervals.

And then something happened. Something almost impossible to explain. For I definitely don't believe in ghosts or supernatural phenomena. But was it just a creaking of the timbers that I heard — or could that faintest sigh of wind have been the breathing of another human being? I couldn't tell. Amongst the dusty cobwebs, the mouldy straw and the crumbled white mortar of the loft whose weatherboarded side was continually being scratched by the kisky twigs of an elderberry shrub, it was difficult to be certain. Indeed, I have never really known what actually alerted me to that *mysterious* other presence. My body froze. I lay dead still. A cold shiver of the paranormal ran up my spine. As if in defiance of my better sense I was gripped by a terrifying sensation of alarm. I didn't move for another twenty minutes. Whether this shadowy 'thing' had remained or moved, I did not know. But I could not wait forever. Eventually I had to take the risk.

With aching limbs and straining eyes, I quietly lowered myself on to the ground and glancing continually to the front and rear, scurried forward with back bent low. At the final clump of apple trees I halted; listened; and then clambered over the crumbling garden wall and frantically made for the cart-track hedge. Here, I found an opening by an ash stub and slithered into the ditch. Soon my face was scratched and my hands were torn from the brambles and the dog rose, but as I struggled forwards they were at least a form of camouflage until I could obtain the sanctuary of 'Colonel's Wood'.

The copse which was planted on a sandy hillock was largely

49

Larch, although a few Oaks provided a little variation. More recently — in a fresh attempt to draw the pheasants — Ian Knightley had planted in some snowberry, dogwood and a little laurel. It was across the brook where the blackthorns grew that Henry had set his snares, an hour or so before.

Creeping to a larger laurel bush, I checked the time. There was less than two minutes before our next 'rendezvous by radio'. I was advantageously positioned, for less than 20 yards from where I crouched, ran the sunken cart-track. Anyone patrolling here, I reasoned, would surely do it from a vehicle rather than on foot. Moments later, I heard Knightley's Land Rover approach; Henry had just commenced his tactical review.

"Have reconnoitred the rape. Visibility poor even on the hill. But we're convinced that we can get our hare there. Redhead has retreated for the rifle."

Bandits approaching!" I hissed, as I heard the rumbling chunder of the vehicle slowly squelch and slither along the slippery track. Flinging myself down, I suddenly felt wet; bedraggled and cold; my stomach called out for feeding and despite my 'waterproof' clothing, the wetness of the day and the dampness of the ground, still penetrated chillingly in.

I cursed, and for the first time experienced a tinge of demoralisation. Maybe our previous New Year's Day antics had not been so misguided after all. I waited dejectedly for the emergency C.B. re-call which was pre-arranged to follow five minutes after a crisis. But when we again made contact, it was Henry's voice which was tense and frustrated.

"They're everywhere! We're almost surrounded. But what's worse, the mist is lifting and sun's breaking through."

It might be of value here, to describe Henry and Redhead's previous movements. Upon the accomplishment of the first task, they had retrieved the birds and hidden them in a secret position. (Actually in a hessian bag behind some concrete blocks in semi-dry culvert, where a man would not look and a cat could not enter.) Then, witnessing the pandemonium around Kings Hall, they had quickly proceeded to Endings Hill, which this year was established in oilseed rape. It was a bold, adventurous move, for the field was like an isthmus of the farm and within our rules, (which included no trespassing on neighbouring land) offered little chance of escape in the event of detection.

Yet despite the sogginess of the rape leaves — and against any logical explanation — we had often observed the large number of hares it drew. After confirming with their binoculars that their quarry existed, Redhead had slipped off on the one public footpath from Endings Hill to our borrowed vehicle, with its rifle and supplies (and which had been left at Dick Hudson's house the night before.)

Now this is how things stood. Redhead had reached the vehicle and was waiting for Henry's instructions. But Henry required another diversion to draw Knightley's patrols from the Wenington roadway before he could give Redhead the signal to advance.

It was 12.35. Already the delights of a long warm bath; of a hot tea and whisky; of clean sheets and dry clothes were ingratiating themselves into my mind like an idyllic and sublimely sweet dream.

"I'd love a flask of soup and a ham and mustard sandwich," I moaned hungrily.

"When you've finished playing John Macnab!" came Henry's rasping reply.

I looked up through the laurel and the larches and between that mixture of hazel and snowberry which was intended to stop the wind and keep the 'bottom' warm for pheasants. Shafts of sunlight were beginning to percolate hazily through the cloudy afternoon; by the steep banked ditch, the thick elder and hazel stubs rose up, not coppiced now these thirty years. Beside them the hornbeam still retained their russett leaves of autumn; closer a crabapple tree protruded, gnarled and crooked and leaning to one side, whilst the bright red stems of dogwood were shining — yes, shining — like polished ruby spindles in a single beam of sunlight.

And then something caught my eye. Out of the far corner some undefined crude shadow seemed to pass too quickly across the dull green wheat of Long Bridge Field behind. On Channel 10, Henry hissed: "No.3; Start!"

"No! I'm under scrutiny I think."

Again I scanned those hazels and that dogwood for some tell-tale sign of a human being observing me. But nothing moved.

We gave it another five minutes. In my seclusion I could

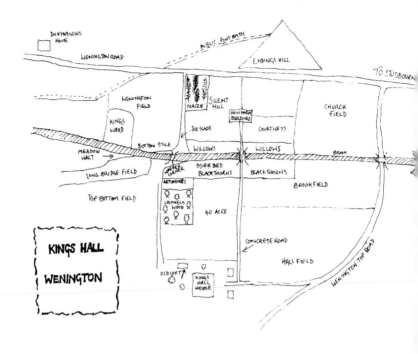

imagine Henry's anxiety. Meanwhile my fears were unconvincing. Both my comrades urged for "Action!" before their hare was lost. And so, outvoted by the others, I was made to move. Creeping through the artichokes, I reached the valley bottom. Here, I leapt perilously across the brook and hauled myself up the slippery bank by the clinging to a branch of sallow.

This time my tactics had to be more sophisticated than before. On the hedge I hung a banger with a five minute fuse rope. Lighting it, I ran along the edge of Silent Hill to Courtney's Field. Crossing the concrete road which links Kings Hall with the new farm buildings, I carefully dropped a little tuft of pheasant feathers and trailed a scent rag along the grass verge where any dog was sure to rummage. Ten yards further on I dropped a couple of 'Ely' twelve-bore shotgun cartridges.

Only then did I come into the open and run uphill towards Endings Field. Deliberately I ensured that the Knightleys saw me. Once certain that I was noticed, I proceeded to feign alarm and seek concealment. But this time they were only duped in part. Only two of their number pursued me but as I led them back towards the brook and where the feathers lay, I saw them stop, their dogs alert and pining as they scrutinized the evidence. Meanwhile I concealed myself amongst the willows. But how fared my companions? Putting the walkie talkie to my ear at 2.15 I was greeted by Henry's exulted, "Success twice over; the diversion was ideally timed!" . . .

Not only, it emerged, had Henry — in the temporary absence of the Knightley team — succeeded in shooting and retrieving a hare, but Redhead had also been successful. Leading a diversionary foray towards the Blackthorns, he had returned to the location of his snares and released a tender rabbit.

We were two-thirds of the way there. And yet for me there was still one nagging moment of misgiving. It had been triggered off when I crossed the track and dropped the feathers. For a pheasant feather or two already lined the drive, and as I crossed the hillock — admittedly out of breath and hungry — I thought that on the further corner of Courtney's Field I had seen a row of sticks. And yes! I knew that it was murky but I was certain that those sticks supported something like a gossamer or net. What on earth were the Knightleys up to?

It would have been pleasant to report that despite the odds which were stacked against us, we successfully concluded the day without panic. By the terms of our wager we had to be finished by half past four. It was now 2.21. We were still the two partridges short.

Initially, Henry and I tried one, rather optimistic attempt at driving a covey over Redhead. We had seen them on Church Field where eight or nine birds often clustered together, but although we came at them from behind, they veered away, yards out of range.

Skirting the roadside hedge, we then made our way down to the Bottom Stile, where we had started in the morning. Here, a long grass slade of forty or fifty yards width, stretched out beside the cart track. It was just the place a partridge might seek refuge on a raw and misty day. With tense impatience, we waited as Henry manoeuvred himself towards the further end to initiate a 'pincer movement of the track'. I glanced at my watch. It was 2.50. "Provided . . . provided," I thought. "Provided that Knightley's patrol doesn't come disturbing us along here for just

53

five minutes more . . . we might still make it!"

Food; warmth; hot baths; strong tea; Ah yes! How these things rose up in my imagination. How much more delightful they would be for their protracted absence!

In the distance I caught sight of Henry stalking warily forward. Alert and checking keenly on either side, he was quietly moving his arms up and down as he goaded the partridge along. Twenty yards to my right, Redhead was doing the same as we cautiously converged. Less than a hundred yards now separated Henry from Redhead and me. Then my ears detected an approaching rumble. It was Knightley's Land Rover. We were thwarted again! Worse, a tractor was coming up behind Henry. Frantically we scurried off to seek safer sanctuaries: Redhead to the new farm buildings; Henry to the dark refuge of Kings Wood and myself — well, I only had a large field with low hedge to give me any security before I reached the willow trees again.

Yet it was whilst we were in this predicament that we had one major piece of luck. For, approaching the greensward behind the new farm buildings, Redhead abruptly noticed a huddled group of red legged partridge squatting on the grass less than fifty yards from the white asbestos barn. He had time for just one quick shot before urgently yelling over Channel 19: "Make a diversion! Make a diversion!" as he retrieved his kill. Henry and I did our best to help him But our limbs were inanimate and cold: and the blood and warmth to revitalise the turgid muscles was thinned down by too many minutes of hiding in cold wet woods and hedgerows. I was chilled to the bone. And unaware of Redhead's full success I began to feel demoralised and apathetic.

We held another C.B. conference and it was Redhead who took a lead and gave command. In my dejected state his plucky quips resounded like a kingly speech to the famished men of Agincourt. We would try another strategy, he said. We would proceed with Tactic 2.

Henry and I both mumbled unenthusiastically, but Redhead's gutteral voice declared; "Pull yourselves together and make a start!"

And so it was I blew my firemans whistle; Redhead's dog went bounding out in full view of Knightley's team to retrieve a piece of wood, and Henry fired his shotgun twice. I answered with the starting pistol and we both produced a cacophony on our whistles. Meanwhile I struggled across the bottom of Courtney's Field and then waited until the headlights of the approaching Land Rover lit up the dummy pheasant that I carried. Again attempting to lead them on, I repeatedly glanced back across my shoulder with a hunted, haunted and exhausted look. It wasn't hard to act.

Reaching the Wenington Brook, I lurched across the concrete bridge and then lumbered towards the tangled Blackthorn Copse. Here a man could hide himself for weeks on end. Behind, I could hear the thwarted attempts of pursuit, but I carried on, weaving beneath and between the thickets until completely secluded.

In the gloaming — maybe 20 yards away from where I halted — was one of Len's feeding troughs. As I searched and scanned ahead, and once or twice behind, I was intrigued to notice a wire 'rat snare' cunningly concealed beside the feeder. I was baffled. For the snare might have also caught a pheasant — the very bird whose survival the feeder was meant to be ensuring. Suddenly Henry's voice broke through my thoughts on Channel 19.

"Number Three. Do you read me?"

"Yes," I hissed.

"Great luck; I've got the brace."

"How?"

"Knightley's team literally drove them over me. Amazing luck! Are you still there?"

"Yes."

"Right. As soon as possible, try to make the rendezvous. Redhead will have the brace of partridge, I'll bring the rabbit and the hare, but you must collect the pheasants. We'll be waiting with the vehicle."

"Over and out," I answered jubilantly, as adrenalin surged through my body.

In the duskiness, I crept slowly towards the feeder. I hadn't far to go now. It was 3.45. There was still just time to complete the challenge. Caution was the imperative word.

But then, as I reached the clearing, I felt it again. That quite curious and terrifying sensation which comes as little goose pimples rise over one's body: when, without reason, your back feels suddenly cold and you look nervously round as if someone is following you when nobody is. It is that unnerving feeling of being observed by something that you cannot see; It is as if an alert sixth sense is conscious of an invisible presence. I felt chilled and nervous, and — if I admit it — a little bit frightened by the hypnotic power of this illusory 'thing'.

"Pull yourself together, do!" I muttered brusquely. But for the next few minutes, I moved as swiftly as I could along the dense, thorn encroached track and when I emerged at the Warren Corner, it was with a sigh of relief at being in open country once again.

From the Warren Corner to the culvert beside Kings Wood, where the pheasants were hidden, was only a few hundred yards. Another ten minutes or so took me from the culvert to the borrowed vehicle and with the darkness increasing every moment, the last jolting hike passed off without incident.

When I arrived at the Escort van, Henry and Redhead were already ensconced and sipping a cup of steaming tea. Henry gazed at me as if I were an apparition and exclaimed joyfully, "Well met brother scarecrow!" I looked at the other two and chuckled at our dishevelled appearance. Each of us had mud-caked hands and knees; our clothes were stained with grass and straw; prickly burdocks clung to our hair and hats; tiny drops of misty rain covered our waterproofs; and little lines of dried blood criss-crossed our faces where we had done battle with a bramble, a blackthorn or a dog rose.

"We can just make it," said Henry, glancing at his watch. It was 4.15. Even as we spoke, Redhead was clambering into the rear of the van.

Jumping into the front, I picked up the brace of partridge, the rabbit and the hare. Onto the partridge was attached a brief message.

To avoid detection Henry drove with side lights alone and as he swung the rickety vehicle around the S-bends and corners of Wenington's narrow lanes, he stared forward with a fixed and straining concentration. Behind him Redhead collected up the dummy creatures. On this occasion it was he who was to act as the decoy.

We approached Kings Hall from the 'Top' road, and as we turned on to the private drive, Henry dowsed the lights. The approach slopes gently down to the Hall. Henry switched off the engine and we coasted quietly down the incline. Nearing the gardener's lodge, Redhead lithely disembarked from the moving vehicle and 'stood by' to create a commotion if a contingency should arise.

Kings Hall itself was lit by four large floodlights. We could see no sign of the opposition. Ours was an audacious move! The Escort had left the concrete now and lost momentum as it crunched on to the gravel drive. Henry quickly turned the ignition key. Alerted by the sound, voices began to shout. Accelerating hard, Henry swung the van round until it was directly in front of the classically pillared porch and less than two yards from the great oak door which was bedecked with a Christmas wreath and an elaborate brass knocker.

Leaping out of the van, a siren started wailing and a bell began to ring; Justin was yelling hoarsely — "They're here! Close the front gate! Close the front gate!"

Across the forecourt, I saw Redhead running coyly before them and in full view, appear to drop a brace of pheasants and then to fumble as he picked them up. His was a superb performance.

"It's Redhead!" someone shouted. "Stop him, he mustn't reach the Garden door!"

"No!" came a counter command. "It's a blind! Quick! Front of the house. Quick! Front!"

"Drop them! Drop them!" Henry was shrieking at me in fury. "Drop them," he yelled maniacally again.

*　　*　　*

I couldn't. Or rather, I could. But only in slow motion. For I was the first one who actually saw it. Bathed in the glow of the orange light from above the door. So simply displayed.

And in that instant everything flashed through my mind. And made sense. That moment of fear in the tumbledown barn; the sensation of having been observed all day; the shadows in the depths of the blackthorn canopy; the misplaced rat snare and the sight of a faraway net on a fog-laiden field.

"Drop them!" roared Henry again.

I turned, almost demented. I tried to speak but my mouth wouldn't move. I tried to explain, but my voice was dumb.

For there — there — beneath me on the stone steps of Kings

Hall, there *already* lay; a brace of pheasants, a brace of partridge; a rabbit and a hare.

Then in the yellowish light, I saw the message. It was attached to the neck of the uppermost pheasant. It was inscribed on the back of an old brown luggage label and it was written with the long loop letters of a *Victorian* education.

"From yours – and with honour at last."
Jonathon Macnab.

HOPPY'S
LAST MATCH

T he envelope had a Somerset postmark. It had been stamped by a franking machine and bore the name of a West Country legal practice. Opening it, I unfolded the stiff, heavy duty letter with interest. The relevant sentences read:

Am arranging a cricket tour of Suffolk in June. We call ourselves 'The Travelling Players' but are actually all professional people from the Taunton area. Any chance of a game? The ninth would be ideal.

The signature at the bottom was familiar. It was Neville Henderson-Smith. I remembered him as a class mate from school. Yes, he would be the prefectorial sort to become a solicitor.

Later that May evening I allowed myself to be convinced that his team of young, varsity educated 'professional people' would not overwhelm my rag-bag band of local farmers and friends.

"Don't worry, he pattered over the telephone. "There are actually only ten of us. Our eleventh player will be my twelve year old brother, Augustine — it's his half term that weekend."

*   *   *

As usual, when you get up a scratch team or party for any event, there is always somebody who drops out at the last minute. In this case it was mid-morning when the 'phone rang and Holston car mechanic, Simon Brown, informed me that he couldn't play.

Despite all attempts I was unable to find a replacement. Finally — and with some embarrassment — I drove across to Hoppy Whelcroft's retirement bungalow. It was a pretty tall order. The old horseman-farmworker had not played circket regularly for nearly fifteen years. Just once — again to make up numbers — he had turned out for the village side when he was sixty seven, yet even that was eight long years ago. But despite all that, I have never known a man of seventy-five to be so youthful, young at heart and willing to join in with any parish activity.

Even so, I almost didn't get out of the car. It really was rather absurd. Disturbing a seventy-five year old man at twelve o'clock on a Sunday morning and suggesting a game of cricket in two hours time! I deserved to be laughed at.

But Hoppy only slowly shook his head: "Years ago I'd have loved to," he smiled, "but I haven't played for such a time . . . surely there must be someone younger."

Obviously I didn't press the point. Besides, his eight year old grandson was listening to our conversation with a face a thousandfold more persuasive than any words that I could muster.

*　　*　　*

The boy just tipped the scales in my favour. For at ten minutes to two, he excitedly informed me of his grandfather's change of mind. Naturally, I was delighted. The feeling of elation endured for just one moment. And then it hit me.

"Oh, my God!" I thought. "What if he gets hit by a ball!" In an instant, a dozen morbid scenes flashed before me. Of the old man overcome with heat when fielding on the boundary: of the panting pensioner running for a ball and suddenly collapsing: of the siren of the ambulance as we stand around in stupified dismay as the old man feels his heart . . . his heart . . . his heart.

But my concern for Hoppy Whelcroft was not merely that of a cricket captain for an older player. It went far deeper. You see I had known him all of my working life. More importantly,

60

through all of the chronic disappointments and headstrong blunders of my youth, it was his quietly guiding voice which had never unnecessarily condemned or sneered.

He was a kind man. Thoughtful and straightforward. Physically strong yet nimble and never a pound overweight. His head wore a mop of silvery hair and his face was stamped with the kindness of cheerful good humour. Cheerfulness! Yes, that was his greatest attribute of all. Even the grimmest and roughest conditions were made a little less onerous by one of his wry comments. For his was the special humour: the dry, sustaining, fortifying humour of Suffolk that generations of land workers have used to lubricate their frugal, poverty-ridden and exploited lives since Suffolk of itself began.

It was from such a family, whose sons had been both horseman and stock-keepers for centuries past, that Hoppy was descended until finally, with the coming of mechanisation, he had become the last of the genuine old horse-keepers to work on the farm.

*   *   *

It was intriguing to meet Neville Henderson-Smith after almost twelve years. He was stouter than when I remember him as a schoolboy and, like his team-mates, had become possessed of a somewhat serious approach to the job in hand. The 'Travelling Players' arrived in well groomed cars with smart wives and scampering children who would soon be at fee paying primaries. The team also contained two doctors.

"Just in case your agricultural fast bowlers crack our ribs!" quipped Neville with a laugh.

We only really made a match of it because John Shepard, Bert Yule and Tommy Smith, who often played for Studbourne Seconds, and John Barnard from Castleton were with us. From the first over it was obvious that the visitors were a class above our rag-tag team of builders, self-employed carpenters, young farm students, beery farmers . . . and Hoppy Whelcroft.

The two Johns and Tommy did almost all the bowling and with our energetic — if chaotic — fielding (overthrows and extras accumulated a good score!), their teatime score of 196 for 3 was still just within the bounds of honour.

Even so, as we trooped off from the pitch and then walked along the road beneath the chestnuts to the village hall, we must have looked a motley bunch. One fielder was sporting coloured plimsolls, two had black trousers, several wore jeans, and another was attired in a bright check shirt.

I sat down next to Sandra Henderson-Smith, Neville's charming and attractive wife. It was easy to imagine her, five or ten years hence, as the perfect candidate's wife at a General Election, or the enchanting Mayoress or Madam Chairman at any function.

On the opposite side of the long 'collapsible' table sat Augustine. Despite not having batted, he still consumed his tea with a voracious appetite. In between enormous mouthfuls of jam sandwiches, however, I learned that he was fascinated by cricket and was otherwise engrossed in a childish passion for collecting stag beetles, birdwatching and conducting smelly experiments with a chemistry set in his bedroom. I asked him once about the beetles. Instantly he gabbled off a string of sub-species by the hundred. It was almost five minutes before I could interrupt and gently make my exit.

Collecting up a *Kit-Kat*, I sauntered outside. On the pavement the studs of my cricket boots made a militaristic 'clack! clack! clack!' whilst behind me the red brick tower of the Parish Church rose up, embalmed in glorious evening sunlight.

Ambling back I passed an elderberry bush so heavily bedecked with flowers that the branches sagged beneath the stunning burden of their brilliant white florescence. Yes I reflected, this was June. *'High June'*! The month of gorgeous white across the countryside. The rampant white of elderflower in meadow hedgerows; the stretching white of cow parsley along the lanes, the white of butterflies and of hawthorn blossom and the white and speckled pink of the 'candles' on the chestnuts around our pitch.

At the far corner, I reached the wooden 'Coronation' bench

where Hoppy, his wife, and heroising grandson were finishing a flask of tea. I gave the boy the *Kit-Kat*.

"Do you think we can win?" he asked optimistically.

I smiled at Hoppy. The toe caps were worn thin on his ancient boots; he was wearing his best white shirt and a pair of baggy black trousers which were all that remained of a pre-war suit. His cricket pullover had aged with time to a custard yellow and was knotted around his waist. Together we idled round to the low green hut that served as our pavilion.

"You were a bit short of bowlers." He summed up. "They almost began to get away with it at times."

Throughout the afternoon Hoppy had fielded at either 'fine leg', 'third man' or 'long on' to save him from journeying too far between the overs yet he had still walked keenly in with each delivery.

As the game resumed and our opening pair marched out to 'the square', we sat down on a wooden form in front of the pavilion and the old man reminisced of the village cricket of his youth.

"I first played here sixty three years ago! I was twelve years old then, about the same age as that 'ere boy, fielding at 'mid on'. Course, we didn't get such big totals that time of day. Maybe we'd be all out for 15 or 20. But we always enjoyed it. And there was 'hell and all' of a competition to get into the side. More's the point, we had all done a full day's work with horses or at hoeing beet or mangels first, and we often had to walk or bike for miles to get a game, but we still used to play on Wednesday nights as well." He paused and chuckled slightly, "I remember one time . . ."

He was interrupted as our first wicket fell to a chorus of excited shouts. Our number three picked up his bat and Hoppy resumed: "That must have been about 1925. We had all biked across to Wenington one Wednesday evening. Now, in those days, their pitch was one of the worst around. There were humps and holes a foot deep on the actual 'square' and enormous docks and thistles on the outfield. Anyway, old Grunty Johnson was in our team and, as usual, he always had to be a cut above the rest of us so he had bought himself a proper set of whites. Well, time we were fielding, old 'Barrell' Norman — the old stallion leader years ago — hit an almighty six and it landed in the brook where the mud was two or three feet deep. Well, what wasn't mud was probably cow pats. Course, no-one volunteered to get balmed up in retrieving the ball, and so we all got on to Grunty and said that being as he was the nearest fielder, then he should go. Well, he wouldn't have none of that — not in his fancy togs — so come the finish, old Dan Riches the blacksmith made us all pick straws. Well, as fortune had it, Grunty Johnson got the task. Course, he was riled as hell, being as he reckoned himself to be so smart and well turned out. I needn't tell you — but he had mud up to his waist by the time he'd finished. 'Why don't you take your trousers off?' someone yelled.

"'Because one of you lot would pinch 'em', he replied, 'and I ain't going to bike home in my underpants!'

"That's funny, though, because years later I said to old Riches one night in *The Bells*, 'How did you arrange it so that Grunty got the short straw?'. He looked over his shoulder and winked. 'I didn't,' he laughed, 'All the straws were the same length! But I just made sure that Grunty choose last. You were second from last if I remember right and of course, when he saw that you had a long straw, he just assumed that the other was short!'".

As the game proceeded, I took a bundle of old score books from the bottom of the pavilion locker and we browsed through them together. Sitting in the evening sunshine and turning the pages of those yellowing, dog-eared and time-stained records, the old man invested each bygone match with a human memory.

"That was a rum old game," he muttered, of a Saturday afternoon in the early May of 1931 when two villages were both bowled out for single figures. " . . . and he was an old devil!" he chuckled, pointing to the name of a thick-set, swarthy threshing machine driver, who had scored 44 without ever moving from his crease.

We turned the pages backwards, working in the reverse order as one sometimes does with fascinating material until Hoppy saw again the details of a match in '28, which was played at a village between Studbourne and Hoston.

"That was a 'tidy' pitch!" he exclaimed. "The land was so

blessed light that there was sand at the surface and the outfield was like a bloomin' rabbit warren. Well, Roosty Hengrave hit one up and it fell down right into one of these 'ere holes. Course you can only officially claim a six for a lost ball, but he made old 'Lightweight' Ginger run a twenty. Poor old 'Lightweight'! He went nearly eighteen stone. It nearly killed the poor beggar. Oh no! He never played no more."

*   *   *

I would have enjoyed reminiscing for longer but out on the square our own game was fast deteriorating and at one point we had lost three wickets for a score of only ten runs. Thankfully the three Studbourne men all got into double figures and when, after witnessing the ferocity of their bowling, I hesitantly walked to the wicket, our score of 70 for 6 at least suggested that we had made a match of it. Fifty minutes of play remained and it was with 'trench warfare' tenacity that the farmers rearguard of Henderson, Rawson and myself slowly prodded and pushed a run here and there until when Rawson was l.b.w. at 6.25 we were 85 for 8.

Robson, the Castleton bowler, was our next man in at number ten. But his reputation was always with the ball and never as a batsman; he lasted until the final ball of the over when a devastating delivery from the Yeovil dentist shattered his stumps in confusion.

*   *   *

A maroon red ray of evening sunlight beamed onto the front of the pavilion; the bells of Hestup Church tolled the last resounding call for Evensong; the rooks flew up two or three at a time from the branches of the firs and dying elms; some children played on the squeaky swings; a young lady walked idly by with a pram; and a teenage boy in a leather jacket sauntered off with his girlfriend to walk in the woods and become one with the stirrings of nature.

Stooping very slightly from a back that was no longer straight, Hoppy emerged from the pavilion. With a grandfather's understanding of all the insignificant things in life that alone make life worth living, he slowly made his way to the wicket. On the boundary, an eight year old boy watched with a face of rapturous excitement.

On the 'square', I caught Neville's eye. My anxiety of Hoppy facing such wanton speed was eased when he quietly muttered, "You're facing the next over. We'll see how it goes."

Six balls later, I hadn't been able to get the single I needed to protect Hoppy from the bowling. At the far end I watched Neville toss the ball from one hand to the other. For a desperate second I was about to protest. Then he lobbed the ball to his twelve year old brother.

Relieved, I glanced at the clock on the church tower. It was half past six. There were thirty minutes to the close of play.

It would be impossible to describe the events of the next half hour. As the old man drew guard and slowly scrutinized the field, whilst at the other end the lanky boy – 'a spinner with a touch of swing' – as he had imaginatively described himself at teatime, placed his soft, slim fingers over the seam of the ball, exactly as he had copied it from his favourite coaching book and studiously marked out his run.

He couldn't always master line and length or true direction, for that is the consistency that comes with age, but he certainly varied his speed and occasionally interposed a leg-break into his sequence. Similarly, he suggested cunning movements of the fielders as he concocted a plethora of schemes of bowling for a catch or maybe for a stumping or possibly a 'leg before'.

But Hoppy at the other end was, with a shuffle or a mis-hit, with a pushing prod or mistimed block, just able to defend his wicket.

I can't remember much of my innings. Once or twice I was able to run a 'two' and keep the bowling as it was. But that itself became quite secondary to the other struggle taking place.

How can I ever describe the tension and emotion that I felt watching the desperate contest that was being staged before us? For in every stroke that he played, I saw Hoppy invest his lifetime's experience and all of his faltering skill. And in each delivery that was bowled, Augustine committed every fibre of his innocent body and every iota of his schoolboy's mind to capturing the old man's wicket.

The initiative ebbed and flowed from the old man to the youngster and then back again. For half an 'over' I thought that Augustine would have him; Hoppy fumbled and nearly got bowled and the next delivery can only have been the merest fraction from skimming leg stump. And then mysteriously his concentration returned, his timing improved, his confidence grew, he almost got Augustine away for a run and the lad showed signs of becoming dispirited at the lack of success. But already it was the end of the over. The contest would soon start again.

It was a sacred battle that I saw out there. It was the struggle between a man who for years on end had trudged behind a horse to plough his 'acre a day', and whose hands had thatched stacks and whose arms had pitched sheaves and whose wrists had pulled beet and whose back had carried the great 'comb' sacks and who was now in his seventy fifth year: and against him were the supple fingers that programmed a home computer, the keen eyes that identified and dissected with microscope and scalpel, the soft hands that played with pipettes and bunsen burners and the career that would only ever be scientific and sedantry.

And it is a curious thing. But I have followed cricket from my earliest days. I was there at the Oval when Trueman took his

300th Test wicket; I've seen Gower and Sobers at Chelmsford and Colchester; I've seen Viv Richards crack a double century in three hours before tea; I can say to my grandchildren that I watched Lillie bowl and Knott 'keep' and Botham at his best.

And with *this* enthusiasm for the game, how can I ever explain that a 0 NOT OUT: and 0 wickets for 0 runs was the most memorable cricket that I have ever witnessed?

*   *   *

Slowly the shadows from the trees began to lengthen. The rich evening sunshine lit up the dark greens of the wheat fields whilst a languid breeze blew waves across the purple-white avils of the winter barley. Yet so pre-occupied were my thoughts that I scarcely noticed the clock creeping closer to seven o'clock.

And then I wondered. *If* I was to face the last ball of play with the result still to be decided, what in all decency should I do? I like to think that I might have been honourable and deliberately broken my stumps.

As it was, no dilemma ensued. For on the first ball of the last over, the Yeovil dentist produced a rocketing away swinger. It was one of those magnificent, unplayable deliveries and I was easily caught by Neville in the slips.

I waited for Hoppy to join me from the other end and together, and rather slowly, I walked beside him towards the hut.

It is possible that amongst the half dozen cars parked on the green the incident that followed occurred without notice. And because there was no Bailey or Johnston or B.B.C. commentator to describe the moment, it might have passed by unrecorded for ever.

But it did happen — simply and quietly — without a word or a sign or a nod or a gesture. Yes, it happened. That a Harley Street doctor in the making; an aspiring politician who has already held ministerial rank, and a future director of the B.B.C. stood back in a line and removed their caps and applauded the innings of an ageing farmworker, and only a schoolboy had to be quietly restrained to let the old man go in on his own.

MOONLIGHT

"That's 'Him'," muttered the thickset farmworker with the ruddy face and faded tweed jacket. We were sitting in a flint walled public house some several miles north of Abbeyford St. Mary. For a Friday evening the public bar was unusually quiet. A couple of regulars sat by the fire warming themselves from the late November chill; a teenager in a leather jacket played a fruit machine indifferently ignoring the plain-faced girl who impassively watched him; a small family group clustered round another table and apart from 'him' there was nobody else but Harry and me.

'Him' and Harry were both aged about sixty five and had been born and schooled in the same village; ("least that's if 'Ee' ever went to school — he was always about in the woods and hardly ever attended from what I can remember"). But whilst Harry had a wide, good-natured face and stood a good six foot tall, "him" was about three inches shorter and bore the appearance of a wiry hardiness. Watching "him" I also noticed that he was permanently alert and through the open bar maintained a cautious watch of who was in the saloon lounge.

Although short and lean he looked strong and fit. For a man of his age he had a good head of chestnut hair and a face that could well have been some ten years younger. He was wearing an old threadbare jacket with a couple of rubber bands for buttons and stitching which was a good deal remiss around the collar. Through the lapel protruded a dull chromium watch chain whilst his cap bulged from one pocket. Beneath the jacket was an unkempt pullover and an open brown shirt. Ageing corduroy trousers tucked inside black Wellington boots, completed his attire.

I suppose that staring at people is one of the faults for which I am often criticised, but I also noticed one other quirk. One of those dodges that detective films still overdo, yet with a jolt I realised why he stood — exactly where he did — by the side of the bar, with one hand resting on the jukebox. For it enabled him, unobtrusively, to glance at the mirror that stands at the back of the liqueur bottles: from this vantage point he could watch the whole room on a busy evening. And with embarrassment as I stared, I caught the reflection of his eye observing everything I did.

Harry rose to buy another round. Approaching the bar, the outside door opened.

"Hello Turnip" he beamed.

"Ev'nin' Harry," uttered the newcomer.

"Ev'nin' Moonlight," he muttered quietly to "Him" as Harry paid for the drinks.

"By the way," he continued, "the old colonel's having a shoot on Wednesday week . . . and he wanted to make sure that you knew".

Moonlight nodded. He seemed to place great value on his words. As if they cost him a lot of money. When he finally spoke it was without tone or expression.

"That's hardly of any interest to a law abider like me." He squinted up at the clock, glanced around the room, and put his empty mug on the top of the jukebox. Out was plucked his dirty brown hat.

"Just off to work are we, Moonlight?" exclaimed Turnip. Moonlight pulled the hat firmly onto his head. He made no attempt to reply. But looking defiant — and yet curiously superior — he momentarily looked Turnip straight in the eye.

Then dismissively shaking his head, he pushed his way to the door and departed.

"He's still a rum devil." said Turnip.

"Doesn't change a bit," agreed Harry.

Noticing my enquiring look he continued without prompting. "The whole family have been like it for years you see. Get a misty sort of night, with just a little moon for light and a gentle wind to confuse the birds' sense of hearing, then I don't believe that he could resist it, even if he was a millionaire. Runs in the blood, that sort of thing."

"But why should the old colonel give him the wink about his shoots?" I asked.

Harry sighed and met Turnip's eye before speaking:

"That's a long story."

"To cut it short," interrupted Turnip, "It's a bit like – well, how shall I put it – it's a bit like as if Moonlight was the official poacher on some of the land around here. I know that sounds daft, but the colonel reckons he can stand what Moonlight takes. In fact I don't suppose it's much more than a brace or two every now and then; but what he can't afford is when these big London gangs come down from the East End with their 'walkie-talkies' and vehicles in waiting and then cream off 20 or 30 brace in one night."

"There was even an incident a couple of years back," added Harry, when Moonlight was 'out' and he came across one of these gangs and he reported them to the police – and there were no questions at all as to how he chanced to come across them."

"To be fair", said Turnip, "I don't expect Moonlight takes as much in a whole season as a London outfit swipe in one night's work. Besides, he always leaves the place alone for a week or so before each shoot. It's like an unwritten agreement."

Intrigued by this oddly symbiotic relationship, I couldn't help asking why the Colonel had never taken Moonlight to court. Turnip looked at Harry before answering and a deep frown passed over his forehead.

"I don't rightly know," he began, "but it would be very difficult to catch him. He can almost look like darkness in the night-time: No, they could spend months – years – worrying themselves silly and waiting up at night and patrolling the estate and still not be able to pin anything on him."

Then Harry cleared his throat. His eyes had taken on a glazed and faraway look as if pre-occupied with some inner problem.

"There is another reason as well."

Turnip nodded and gazed across the empty pub, so lost in thought and suddenly so heavy in spirit that for some moments I dared not interrupt.

It seemed a good juncture to refill our glasses, but even after I had placed the full mugs down on the Greene King beer mats, the mood did not change.

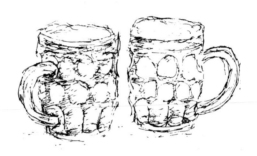

The moments passed slowly by. We sat in silence. Feeling awkward, I stared at the fire.

Finally Turnip murmured sadly.

"He was a rum bugger. Even then."

"He's never changed."

"Remember that first day in the barracks?"

"Should think I do!"

"Poor old Moonlight."

"Like you say, it runs in the family. None of them had ever been proper 'regular' people and suddenly there he was, dressed up in a uniform, having to conform to the army way of life and being hollered at by Sergeant Major Sneezum.

"'I'll make a soldier out of you, Moonlight', he had bellowed in front of the whole company. 'You'll learn some discipline while you're here.' 'Lights out' is at ten o'clock sharp Moonlight! No more night-time excursions for you, my lad.' And Moonlight looked him right back in the eye. He never said a word. Of course, he wasn't allowed to; but I was standing two places from him and there was a look in his eye which seemed to say, 'I'll get even with you one day, Mr. Sneezum.' But I didn't see any more because Sneezum hollered out, 'Eyes forward, Hawkins!' and of course we had to do what we were told.

"But poor ol' Moonlight! He almost faded away time we were in Barracks. It was like watching a wild animal that goes out of condition because it can't stand captivity. Moonlight was like that. He hardly ever spoke at the best of times, but now it was even worse. You'd see him brooding for hours on end whilst he tended an old jackdaw with a broken wing, or simply fretting to himself if he heard a cock bird call in the distance. I sometimes think he'd have gone completely downhill if it hadn't been for his oath to get even with the Sar' Major.

"Anyway, it was on the boat it happened. The *S.S. Strathlaird*, I think the name was. You see, we had all been trundled off to Liverpool and put on this 'ere boat which was bound for hell knows where. I mean, the Army didn't tell you where you were going. It could have been anywhere. Egypt, Gold Coast, Middle East or India. We didn't actually know that it was to be Singapore, until we were past The Cape, and some of the old sweats reckoned that they could see Bombay again. Still, that's beside the point."

"Blasted rum 'en" said Turnip. "To think we went half way round the world without actually knowing where we were destined."

"It was awful," resumed Harry. "Everything was awful. I mean, we were crammed on that boat like sardines. It was meant to accommodate 2000 people, but there was over six thousand of us on that troopship. We hardly had room to breathe or think but that's where Moonlight got his own back, cunning blighter that he is."

"What actually happened was this," explained Turnip. "Moonlight found out where the Sergeant Major's quarters were. And not long after, the Sar' Major discovered that he had a problem." He emphasised the last few words and then deliberately paused.

"What was that?" I asked. Turnip grimmaced and his cheeks went tight.

"Rats," he hissed. "That was the Sergeant Major's problem." He pointed a thick and rough nailed finger at me. "And mighty curious it was too. For the only place on that whole ship where they congregated so, was Sneezum's cabin. Come the finish it got so bad that whatever the Sar' Major did, these rats kept reappearing. They were just crazy to get in. He blocked up every gap and chink but they still kept on. They gnawed fresh holes, came up from beneath the deck, nibbled the chipboard beside the pipes or crept in if the Sergeant Major's door was left open ... or got opened by somebody else! – Well, I don't reckon Sneezum slept at all for about a week, on account of these rats. Of course, he knew all about Moonlight and he soon figured things out for himself. So, one morning during P.T., he announced that he had received several complaints about the overcrowded conditions in the men's quarters and because he wished to experience them at first hand, he had arranged to spend the rest of the journey 'below decks'. However, since all the hammocks were already accounted for he would swap with one of the privates who could have his cabin. Not surprisingly there was a pretty mixed reaction to this suggestion. Those of us who knew about the rats were horrified. But the rest of 'em reckoned it was a famous idea. The Sergeant Major paused for a moment and then someone asked him:

'"How is the 'lucky' man going to be selected?'

'I've already done it,' the Sar' Major answered.

'How?'

'I took a pin; shut my eyes and stuck it into the battalion muster list.'

'Whose name did you pick?' several wanted to know. Course, all the while Sneezum played along like an actor in this little game. And then he roared, 'Moonlight! That's right! You Moonlight: You can have the *privelege* of my cabin 'til this journey ends.'"

"Well, Moonlight never said a word. He didn't even react at all. Impassive as a rock, he is." Turnip paused again and we waited for the twist; "But – I – can – tell – you," he concluded. "Moonlight never once went short of sleep. Oh no. He never complained of rats in that cabin. Old Moonlight – he was a cunning, cunning rogue."

There was another break in our conversation. The public house was more crowded now, and the increasing background noise made it easier to talk in confidence. But when Harry resumed, it was to say something which really surprised me.

"Come the finish," he said gravely, "the old Sar' Major and a hell of a lot more besides, came to almost worship Moonlight."

Harry spoke with such utter – total – sadness, that I felt it was insensitive to further probe his memories. Instead — and tantalized — I waited for the two old friends to carry the conversation forward. But neither spoke.

Again the moments ticked past. Again I wondered disappointedly if their memories were to remain locked behind an impenetrable barrier. Then Turnip looked at me. There was a tightness around his lips and his words were fierce and bitter.

"You've heard about the collapse of Singapore?"

I nodded. Yes, I had heard about it before: That terrible story of the young volunteers in the local regiments who in January 1942 had been sent half-way round the world to be landed on the Malay peninsular and within a fortnight be marched into Japanese Prisoner of War camps for three and a half years.

Harry, with his robust open face, seemed to find it a little easier to recall than Turnip.

"They took us to Changi first — that's in Singapore itself — and then in time they moved us across Malaya and into Thailand. That was an uncanny thing though; even at Changi, old Moonlight got one in.

"You see, after the capitulation we were all crammed in that place and treated something wicked. Talk about stench, filth and hunger — well, in retrospect it was only the beginning — but it seemed bad enough at the time. Anyway, about the tenth day, before it had all become an endless blur, Sar' Major Sneezum — God bless him — tried to protest to the Japanese Officer who inspected us. This Jap officer, he went purple with rage. "English officer only;" he yelled, "only officer rank allowed to make complaint. You only 'other rank'," he screamed, viciously smashing Sneezum's face with the palm of his hand. Then this Nip officer beckoned to three of his soldiers and they bound Sneezum's hands and legs to a bamboo frame and then four of them dragged him in front of us.

"Insolence! Insolence to an officer of the Imperial Japanese Army," the Nipon shrieked. Then he gave the signal. The two front soldiers tore off Sneezum's shirt and thrashed his back with bamboo lathis until it was a mass of lacerated skin and blood. Poor Sneezum. He grit his teeth for all of us. He never moaned, not once. But when they untied him he had already passed out. He never made a whimper. He just crumpled up right there. The Nips just sneered and walked away. We had to carry the poor blighter back.

"And then something fearful happened. Something that's so blessed dark and baffling that I hardly talk about it even now. But I do swear to God Almighty, that I saw it."

Harry was whispering. He looked over each shoulder and his eyes were unsettled and restless.

"Its like this. When they dragged Sneezum back into our hut, that arrogant officer came prancing through, screaming, 'Now! We are the masters! We are the masters!' Well, something awful cunning happened then. Moonlight was standing at the front and he started swaying and when the officer strode by he appeared to faint — and fall upon him.

"Anyway," he continued, "A couple of hours after they half killed the Sar' Major", we had the evening roll call. Now just as we were falling into line, old Moonlight came tearing across the parade ground as if he was a bit on the late side. Matter of fact, you'd have thought he was drunk. He came rushing across and then tripped — arse over head — right over the roots of a big Banyan tree. He screamed out like a demon! Then for just one moment he was out of sight, hidden by the trunk. When he emerged he hobbled towards us, crying aloud and banging an old tin can as if he was a bit simple. Anyway, at that moment, the Japanese officer who had ordered Sneezum's flogging, strode out of the guard house with two subordinates to inspect us. We all stood to attention whilst they three pranced about in front. But Moonlight took a step forward pointing to his foot. Immediately the officer marched across to strike him. Then I noticed something odd. I was staring at my feet to avoid looking at the Nips, when suddenly I heard a furious buzzing and the ground where I stood went dark. I looked up and the biggest swarm of bees that I have ever seen was coming from the banyan tree and hovering overhead. Oh God! They remained there for just a second. Then they just fell onto that Japanese Officer. They were wild and angry and ferocious too. It was hideous. They wouldn't withdraw. This Nip tried to protect himself with his arms, but that only made it worse. He was completely smothered and he was screaming, yelling and shrieking out with pain. You couldn't see him for bees. It was desperate. They would have had him for sure if the other guards hadn't rushed across and flung him into a tank of water."

"Terrible," muttered Turnip.

"And Moonlight didn't even bat an eyelid. He didn't react at all. I think he must be nearly made of stone. And it was never directly mentioned because you never knew if the Nips could overhear your conversations. But when the Sar' Major staggered into the hut after the inspection was over, he paused by Moonlight's bunk and although he never said a word, he stopped for just a second. And his eyes blinked – very, very slowly – just as if he was saying 'thank you' with them. And because my name was only one different to Moonlight's and I was right next to him, I think that what he did was very, very faintly, nod."

Some weeks after this incident the incarcerated soldiers were taken north and divided into working parties. But with the Japanese conquest of Burma, the urgency for railway lines and bridges increased and the prisoners were made to work ever longer hours on smaller rations. Inevitably the physical and mental toll began to tell upon the emaciated, gaunt, and hungry troops in the ragged remnants of their uniforms. Many died from sheer starvation. But — as has been so well chronicled elsewhere, — it wasn't simply those who suffered; it was all those whose resistance to withstand the enervating conditions had finally been exhausted. Those walking skeletons, who were so totally malnourished, that no more reserves remained to fight the dysentary and the diseases, the malaria and the fevers of Asia's jungles and swamps.

That was when Moonlight went to war on his own. In the jungle edges that bordered the camps; by the rivers and pools where they washed; along the beaten tracks where they worked each day; around the perimeter wire of the camp at night; on the grassy banks of the clearing near the bridge; those — those were his battlefields, it was there that he fought his one man campaign.

And month after month as the prisoners were moved from

the limestone hills in the Malayan forests; past abandoned tea estates and rubber plantations; along the wide sands of the Siam coast to the jungles beside the notorious railway; wherever they were pitifully and desperately staking survival, there too, there passed the legend of the short 'tuan' with the squinting eyes. He had a catapult made from an old tyre tube and a fishing line improvised from abandoned wire. He had traps and snares that were all self made but above all, he was fearlessly indifferent to the sounds and shrieks of the jungle. And the native villagers spoke in hushed whispers of his ability to see through the dark of night as they repeated — in awe — one to the other of how he could 'call' the animals and birds towards him at twilight and how he could foretell their movements and blend into their kingdom and become one with their animal world. The 'tuan' with the restless eyes. That's what they named him. He was the one who had bargained a monkey or a snake for a long, wide fishing net, a crate of bananas or a tin of sugar. It was he — the one who never smiled — who had swapped the half dozen jungle birds that were surplus to his comrades needs for a score of hens eggs; or a bushel of rice; or a hat full of lentils or anything else that the 'kampong' had in abundance and was willing to trade.

Yet despite his prowess, Moonlight had remained as private as ever.

"Just occasionally," recalled Harry, "he might get one of us to help him with the ropes and the nets or the snares or the bamboo traps that he set. But mostly he worked on his own . . . and the fact of the matter is this . . . but there were plenty of times when we would all have starved to death if it hadn't been for Moonlight and his secret ways."

"Most of us country boys could do a thing or two," added Turnip, "such as set a snare or use a catapault and so forth — but Moonlight — well, it's exactly as Harry has said, he simply had the 'craft' — like them who had the power over horses — and he was nearly always successful."

"Patience. That's what it was," said Harry. "He had the patience of a stone. I mean, at the start, if we had a rest day, you would see him watching something in the jungle from the perimeter of the camp and at night-time he would still be there. He wouldn't have moved at all . . . and of course, in time he accummulated a lot of knowledge. Well, the guards came to respect him as well and towards the end, they would even let Moonlight go off into the jungle with a rifle and single bullet . . . he hardly ever came back without some bounty."

Harry sighed. It was difficult to imagine two such hearty, well fleshed farm workers ever having been short of food. They seemed to read my thoughts.

"You know, I was less than six stone when I came back," declared Turnip, "and I reckon that despite everything Moonlight did, the two of us together wouldn't weigh as much in total as what either one of us does now."

Harry nodded. He still had some photographs of what he looked like when the war ended as an awful reminder of those times.

"You couldn't recognise yourself!" he exclaimed. "You'd see some bony skeleton staring at you in the mirror and you'd think to yourself, 'who the devil is *that* poor wretch? — and it would be yourself!"

*　　*　　*

It was after the half-starved rabble with Harry, Moonlight and Turnip in their number had been moved up country to slave on the infamous railway line which was being built from Bangkok into Burma, that the tide against the Imperial Japanese Army was reversed. On the 'death railway' itself, the construction schedules became ever more impossible to achieve. The Japanese guards became yet more brutal in their treatment of ill prisoners and demanding of those who lived: Red Cross parcels and medical supplies dried up entirely; and the daily rice ration was reduced again . . . and again . . . and again.

The human misery that was endured during that terrible experience; the suffering of the weak and emaciated soldiers; the dysentary and the lack of hygiene; the terrible stench of death; the hideous sores which developed on the prisoners' debilitated frames; the daily toll of men who collapsed in the heat of the working day with pick or hammer in hand, has been fully recorded elsewhere.

Today, the cemetaries, maintained by the War Graves Commission in Thailand and in Burma, provide still, the final sanctuary of those allied soldiers — so many from East Anglia —

for whom the grace of death was a blissful end to a hideous and fading life.

*   *   *

Turnip picked up our mugs and ordered another round. Harry and I remained in thoughtful silence whilst Turnip placed my shandy on the table; paid the barmaid and returned with half pints for Harry and himself.

After sitting down, he muttered slowly. "We caught up with the Sar' Major once more as well." It was not difficult to foretell his next sentence.

"It was pitiful. He was totally done in. You see, we had just been moved to another camp and when he saw Moonlight and us from the old Regiment come stumbling through the gates, he tried to talk. But he could only gasp out his words in a hollow whisper.

'Moonlight... Moonlight!...' And Moonlight turned to him and the ol' Sar' Major hissed, 'I'll make a soldier out of you yet, Moonlight'. And then he fell back on his grass pillow all exhausted, and Moonlight (and it's the only time I've ever heard him speak so frankly), said quietly, "Hold on, Sar' Major . . . you'll be grateful for my night-time ways as yet.'

"And whether it was because of the extra food that Moonlight caught, I do not know, but for a few days the Sar' Major gave the impression that he might pull through. But then the dysentary came back and swept through the camp just like a forest fire and it took ol' Sneezum and plenty more besides."

*   *   *

Harry got out his pocket watch. Turnip yawned and stretched his arms and legs so that the joints creaked. Raking his big hand through his hair, he gave me a grim smile. But it was Harry who spoke.

"Got to be going home soon. We are lifting beet tomorrow. It's curious though. I hardly wanted to remember all that — everything we've told you tonight — but now we've got it out I feel a lot happier about remembering those times."

And as they got up to 'go home and get ready for the mornin' they each passed a final comment.

"People who were never out there," said Harry, gruffly, "go on about all these medals like the Burma Star and so forth. But I'll tell you this boy. As far as I am concerned it is Moonlight — devious bugger that he is — who is my bloody Burma Star."

Then Turnip spoke — and like on the previous occasions leaned across the table and stared right up to my face as he whispered; "You see; we haven't quite told you everything yet." For a fraction of a second he paused. "But there was somebody else out there with us nearly all the time from Singapore to the Death railway. He wasn't much more than a boy then, about 20 or 21, I expect, and he was a nice lad in his own way – but – well, you see the thing was, he was a bit different to we. He'd had a good education, spoke with a posh accent; parents had plenty of money . . ."

"The fact of the matter," explained Harry, "was that he was an officer . . . mind in those days he was only as junior as you can get . . . but that was the difference."

And so that is why it is, that sometimes on an evening in late November when the night-time sky is pale — but not yet quite a full moon — and there is just a little wind to ruffle up the branches, so that the birds have to grip a little tighter to still hold on, that as he reads beside the fire in the sitting room of _____ Hall, the silver-haired Colonel will sometimes hear that tell-tale 'cuck-cck-cck' of disturbed pheasants calling from the woods or the noisy whirr of their wings as they beat in panic on the wind to make their quick escape.

But at that moment, instead of reaching for the telephone or striding to the Land Rover parked outside, he will instead grimmace and curse, before he gently feels the scars upon his back where a bamboo 'lathi' was beaten some forty years before. Then, sipping another mouthful of the whisky from his crystal tumbler he strokes the golden retriever which sits upon the carpet at his feet and glances at the photograph which stands atop the marble mantlepiece above the fire.

It is of the thirty men in uniform who were the first platoon he officered; his hair was brown and wavy then; and his supple limbs could run the 100 yards in better time than any other soldier in the Battalion. For just a moment, he reflects upon those early years; and then he swears again and mutters with both an irritation and a perverse love.

"God bless you, b_____ Moonlight," he sighs. "Your tricks saved the lives of thirty men — and me — beside the River Kwai."

Part II

BIG AL

T alk of the generation gap? Ask ten young farmers what most annoys them and I'll bet they'll answer.

"Fathers!"

*   *   *

Take mine, for example. Gone seventy — and mad as a March hare.

And the story of Big Al? Well, that just about sums things up. Even though it happened over six years ago . . . in fact on the morning of his sixty-fifth birthday. Yes, *sixty five* . . . the age of retirement.

I was at breakfast and thinking how he would slow down a bit and generally ease off. All of a sudden and what do I hear? The old man tearing down stairs like a rampaging bullock in a springtime meadow.

"Happy Bir . . . " I began, as he burst through the door.

"Guess what I saw last night hidden up in a wood."

"God knows,"

"And old Allis Chambers crawler. Doesn't look like it's run for years. Surrounded by nettles and cowmumble two yards high."

"Oh no." I groaned weakly.

"It's in a spinney, near Hevington, on the Abbeyford road."

"You aren't seriously interested," I said, as an image of our cluttered farm workshop swamped by this redundant tractor, rose in my mind.

"Interested! I'm meeting the farmer who owns it this morning."

"What on earth for?"

"Could be useful; very useful," came the retort. "Even though I'm retired I'll still do all of your 'mole draining' and 'subsoiling' for you. Don't you worry son, I'll soon get the winch and the engine working again."

I knew of course, that he would. All of that wartime generation — men like my father with arms like tree trunks and an intuitive gift for earthy mechanics — have the knack and the ingenuity and the confidence of gross improvisation to make almost anything work. But I also knew that as age took over, there were rather more dreams than accomplished projects. Plenty more talk than actual results. Moreover, I was already embarrassed by our surfeit of old fashioned implements.

"She's an H.D.14," he continued, striding round the kitchen table with the enthusiasm of a schoolboy for a badly tuned motorbike. "An H.D.14! That's 175 horsepower *on tracks!* It's the equivalent of 300 horsepower on rubber wheels! We will have the biggest tractor around here for miles!"

"When it's working."

He ignored me.

"I shall need the chainsaw."

"Chainsaw?"

To cut down the shrubs and bushes around it."

"What the *heck* have you bought?"

"14 ton of solid engineering boy."

"14 ton of scrap metal, more like."

*   *   *

We were both right in a way. It was *totally* siezed up; rusted and

abandoned. There again he didn't pay much more than scrap price for it anyway. And as we cleared the cowmumble and ivy and stamped a track round the veritable colussus, I too felt a discreet and begrudging respect for the big tractor. It was built in 1943 and must have seen service in the war — in the Pacific or 'D-Day' landings perhaps, for beneath the lichen and rust, the old paint flaked off to reveal the brown and green of camouflage. Later on — according to the vendor — "Big Al" — as he called it — had been used on the Ground-nut scheme in East Africa before a long phase of semi-retirement on the clays of his Suffolk farm.

The vendor was a basically fair man. Farmers — like most people — generally are. They might be sharp and fly over a few pounds here and there, and the minutae of a deal but they'd seldom rob a man over thousands or even hundreds.

He even pointed out the major faults before quietly stating, "She's for sale as she stands." They had a little haggle. One invoking the possible potential, the other counting the rings of a sawn down tree ('stood here 12 years at least'); checking the dipstick ('beneath low') and pouring water in the radiator . . . which leaked.

The normal procedure continued; 'be a fool to take less'; 'We might as well leave it'; . . . until in time and of course the bartering progressed, and a deal was struck and a cheque written. My heart sank even further. There was only one consolation.

It required a cross between imagination and fantasy to ever see that old crawler running again. It would probably be in the same wood in ten years time. I didn't hesitate to say so.

Four days later I heard Father ordering a low loader. He had got the engine firing. Big Al was brought to the farm.

That's when the aggravation really began. I was 20 at the time. The 'age' when any ambitious young farmer knows exactly how he wants things to be. And Big Al was always in the way. First of all it broke down in front of the workshop so that on cold wet days we couldn't shut the doors — or get anything else inside. That was while we freed off the track adjusters by squirting in 'Plus-gas' by the gallon and pounding the siezed up 'clamp blocks' with sledge hammers.

After six months we finally had both sides tightened up and with harvest over, we hitched Big Al onto a 'mole drainer'. To be quite fair she made a first rate job on the heavy soil of Old Wood Field. Until the gear cog sheared.

For the next nine months whilst a replacement was precision made and tinkered in, I had to sow and to 'top-dress', to spray and to combine right round that broken down crawler. More to the point, it was the first year that 'I' had begun to do trials work with A.D.A.S. Dozens of local farmers visited the farm and invariably asked, 'What's that thing doing?', and, 'why do your drill lines go round in a circle?'

Eventually Father got it mended and the following autumn finished Old Wood Field and a couple more beside. 'I' might even have thought that Big Al was a worthwhile investment; until he drove it home. A main track sprocket cracked. Just at the back of the Dutch barn. Right in the middle of our main farm road. Well we shoved and crow-barred and hammered and jacked, but it was all to no avail. No — that's not true. We succeeded in time. Dunten determination always does. But it was time as well. For three months that autumn we had to detour from the stone track and across the squelchy field with every pass of tractor and plough, seed corn for the drill and nearly 600 tons of sugar beet on trailers. Oh Hell! There were tracks nearly a yard deep and an acre wide before Al was repaired and moved off the hard standing road.

It was at moments like that when Kenny Knight — the self employed engineer from Fulmer, would drive up and say,

'There's 14 ton of solid metal there . . . '
'Wish you'd sell it for me; I'd respond.

* * *

Finally we got it up to the isolated old barn which 'I' had converted into an implement shed. To be more precise Father drove the crawler through the door. And stopped it. 'We'll move those bales after dinner and I'll swing it right back into the corner and out of the way.'

And after dinner? The atomiser went 90% cuckoo.

"Aren't we lucky it's happened here," he quipped.

"Lucky . . . . .!"

It was just starting to snow. Ruefully, I looked at all the modern machinery that I had worked so hard to acquire. Now it would have to remain outside in the awful wintery weather. As I say, — if there's one thing that annoys you when you're young on a farm — it's Fathers!

Six weeks later, and with the parents on holiday, Kenny Knight rang up.

"Scrap metal's gone through the roof!" he exclaimed. "Get the Allis started. Just move it ten yards onto the concrete road and Bobby Driver will take it away. He will pay double what your old chap gave for it."

I didn't hesitate or have a moments reservation. Things had gone past a joke. Jump leads and booster batteries were placed in the Land Rover alongside spanners and 'Easi-start'. Then I struggled all day and half of the night and most of the following weekend with wire brush, compressor and solvent.

But could I get the damn thing going? Could I get the blasted engine to fire? It was all to no avail. The old devil wouldn't start: Not for me anyway.

A week later the parents returned. Well, I stormed and I swore and we battled and rowed and had a blazing good full-scale set to.

In a filtered way the message got through. Some urgnecy was injected. The atomisers were reconditioned — and Al was manoeuvred into the darkest corner of the old barn.

* * *

And so the years passed and the farm got together and 'I' felt mighty proud of what 'I'd' achieved.

It isn't that I wish to be big-headed. But my generation has done a lot. After all, it was my generation that doubled the yield of wheat. It was we who had built the barns; laid the concrete roads; heated the workshops; purchased tractors with cabs and started to do experimental work on our own farms. Damn it, yes! We have plenty to be proud of.

That's why, 'I' could handle that awful harvest. You remember the year. The worst in living memory. When it didn't stop raining from June to October and on two occasions the streets of Lower Studbourne were two feet under water. The Stud broke its banks; the meadows became lakes; there were landslides in lanes and the Wenington footbridge was half washed away.

But we still had to get in the harvest. The crops were flattened in great swales across the fields; patches of cleavers and chickweed grew through; the wheat began to sprout in the ear; the barley heads fell off; the moisture was never beneath eighteen per cent; yields were desperately low and finally the straw was too wet to burn.

But 'I' could handle it. With the new 'grain drier' and the big barns, with the concrete roads and four-wheel-drive' tractors, with the high-spec combine and my own self confidence, 'I' could take it all in my stride.

It took some effort as well. On the very first field of winter barley, the combine got stuck in a wet boggy patch. For a moment it had me worried. To see the enormous machine up to its axles in mud. But not for long. 'I' simply called up Bob on the C.B. and told him to bring the 180 h.p. T.W. Ford tractor and a big wire rope. It was no problem. No problem at all. We were soon hauled out and harvesting again. But it *was* the bane of that year. Getting stuck. Time and time again it happened – curiously on the light land more than the heavy. But 'I' had the solution. 'I' could handle it all.

Until August 23rd. At the time we didn't know, but it was our last days combining for ten whole days. A week and a half's continuous wet weather. What a harvest!

It was mid morning and I was 'snatching' a few acres on Appleton Field. Soil conditions were greasy and damp; forward traction was difficult and the front 'cutter-bar' continually blocked up with a mixture of torn out barley and mud. I was halfway across – about 200 yards from Higley Wood – when I felt it going. I tried to reverse; too late; I had lost it. We were set again.

"Blast it!"

I called up Bob and waited for him to bring the lumbering 180 h.p. ploughing tractor. When he arrived I hooked on the wire rope as usual. It was just beginning to drizzle.

We followed the standard procedure. He took the strain and I went maximum revs and reverse hydrostatic; the combine began to skew rearwards.

And stuck. I opened the cab door. Twenty yards behind me the giant tractor had bogged down; set deep to its axles. Beneath me now and across the field I could see the water oozing up from where the combines wheels had mangled a land drain into a free running spring.

"Oh Hell!"

"What now?"

"Call up the trailer tractor. We'll pull you out first." My bravado was shaken. But 'I' was still confident. 'I' could handle all odds.

Eric unhitched the trailer and drove over the 115 h.p. tractor. It bogged down. We unhooked its twin to pull out Eric's. It stuck. With a sense of doom – grimly disguised as adventure, I returned to the farmstead, removed the 100 horse Ford 7610 from the headland plough and chained it onto the foremost tractor. One has a premonition of awfulness. As if the spearmen of fate are closing in.

We carefully prodded the ground where the 7610 was to stand. It seemed firm. I signalled to Eric to take the strain.

The 7610 set as well.

Eric clambered out and cursed.

"You'd better get your dinner," I said.

Totally alone I squelched across the cut stubble with the muddy straw sticking to my boots to seek refuge in the combine from the slashing rain.

The adrenalin was gone now. There was no excitement in this. No adventure or conceivable humour. It was unutterably awful. The combine and four tractors stuck in a row over a burst drain and only wet weather to come. I had no more tricks up my sleeve. There was no escape and no way out.

The full weight of despondancy hit me. The dulled thick ache of an awful tiredness enveloped. Whatever we did would take all weekend. Somehow or other I supposed it were possible. We *could* hire another tractor, get a load of railway sleepers, build a solid track and slowly haul out the tractors. And maybe, perhaps in time, we could release the combines 'cutter bar', hire a digger, lift it out of the way, build another causeway of girders and sleepers and drag the combine out forwards.

Yes, I thought starkly, there would be solutions. There always were. But there was no energy left; no oil in my engine; no bodily reserves to call on. For days we had been so tense and so taut. We had worked *so* hard. I glanced up at the combine mirror. A haggard face looked back. It was mine.

God! That those anxiety worn features were on my own twenty-five year old body. My generation!

I dropped my head in my hands and leaned on the steering wheel. I shut my eyes and momentarily tried to sleep, as if sleep would somehow take it away — all the anguish and tiredness; as if the nightmare would end and I would wake up and it wouldn't be happening. I remained for some moments; numbed and defeated and waiting for the strength to return. But there was no panacea. Only a grim awareness of the hours of work that were needed to put it all right.

I lifted my head and it felt like a ton. I gazed through the rain splattered windscreen. A steady stream of water ran off the cab roof. Small pools had formed in the track marks of the previous bout. The rain was heavier now, and as it fell, each puddle became a mass of pock marked craters and holes. My options were lessening by the minute. The storm was closing in. A great arc of lightning lit up the western sky and was followed by a roar of belligerent thunder over Hestup Church. A vivid flash zagged over Fulmer village — through the wierdly grey and sand orange sky — to be followed by a deafening crash. Yet even as it died, there was another retort — continuous and rumbling — from Wenington valley; a sharper crack over Higley Wood; a shattering cannonade from Fulmer again, an approaching rumble from the Studbourne direction; a long, low growl from the old barn way.

A long low growl from the old barn way.

I raised my head slowly; with a peculiar fatalism. Through the slashing rain I could just see it. Emerging in a cloud of silvery black smoke and then creaking slowly, at a snail's pace, across the two fields towards me.

Even at that distance I could discern my father, rain lashed and drenched — for there are no cabs on the old crawlers — as he tugged at the levers with his battered hands, while a little Jack Russell padded in the puddles behind him.

As Big Al approached the downpour increased. I got out of

the combine, dug out the chains and hooked them onto the front of the 7610. The crawler was little more than 'ticking over'. Human reactions *are* impossible at times. I should have said 'saved the day' or 'thanks a million'.

"You must be daft. You'll get pneumonia up there", I snapped crossly instead.

Expressionless, he looked right through me to some indefinite point beyond Higley Wood. I clambered onto the Ford tractor; Big Al took the strain, the cleats bit the soil; the tracks took the weight; we eased forward. The crawler was still 'ticking over'.

Not a word more was said. The procedure was repeated with the two Ford 8210's. But now we were pulling at an 'off centre' angle to avoid the previous wet pits and ruts. Not until we hauled out the big T.W. did father open up Al to about half throttle.

When only the combine remained I dragged out the long wire rope. There was a temporary respite in the storm — but a heavy mist — if you can have such a thing in August, enveloped our earthy struggle. I quickly dug a trench to put the chains around the combine's axle, before shackling them on to the rope.

"Mind your hands on that wire," he muttered.

I glanced at the combine, now sunk even deeper than its chassis.

"This'll make that b_____ crawler bark!" I thought in a perverse moment of bizarre masochism, wierdly half wanting it to fail. Human nature *is* contorted. 'Fourteen ton of solid scrap' flashed derisively through my mind. I couldn't bear to be grateful.

I climbed into the combine and let it warm up before leaning out of the door to give the signal. Father pushed the throttle forward. A great flume of black smoke belched upwards — the old crawler fairly barked out! I slammed the hydrostatic lever into maximum reverse. The rope went taut, Big Al took the strain, the tracks sunk deep; the combine creaked rearwards; the crawler was steady. But we were static again. We had stopped. The combine was sinking. Again Dad's hand hit the throttle. And Al was thundering and roaring and bursting out smoke and we were inching and slipping and sliding and lurching, — the combine was slowly surmounting the 'wall' at the end of its rut!

There was one last pause and then — and then — we were free! Cautiously at first, but with ever more certainty, riding smoothly and evenly under my own motive power, over the stubble of Appleton Field, to the barn at the farm.

By the concrete road we halted. The combine was out! The tractors were out! The nightmare was over!

I sprang from the seat to leap to the ground and cry out with joy and relief.

I just caught myself.

Stiffly I closed the cab door. And slowly and with deliberate movements descended and walked seriously to the rear of the combine.

The old crawler was reversed back, allowing me to release the chain and big 'D-iron'. Gravely and with great concentration, I unhooked and stowed away the shackle and chain.

The big crawler was idling now; with that same gutteral strength that had beat out on the Normandy beaches and African plains. Father sat half turned, watching me work; waiting for the crawler to be unhooked that he might go home and get dry.

With a hammer and pliers I removed the pin from the Allis's draw-bar. At some point I had to hand it up to him. But there was an excuse to delay. It was still half covered with mud. I turned away to clean it, the little boy still battling within.

"Hurry up, do!"

I put the tools away and turned to the crawler, with the pin in my hand. Again I caught sight of the combine and the tractors — all four of them — on dry ground and solid. I was saved! The combine was out! The nightmare *was* over!

Instantly I swung round, took out my handkerchief and pretended to be blowing my nose. I turned again, determined to hold it. I clenched my fist till the knuckles gleamed white and I feared that the bones should snap; I bit my tongue with my teeth so fierce that I thought I should slice it right through. I clamped my jaws together — so tight and so hard — that I felt the teeth should instantly shatter. But in the end I couldn't hold it. Not a moment longer. I just stood there . . . yes, I just stood there . . .

And burst out laughing.

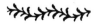

THE CASE OF
THE RABBIT SHOOTING

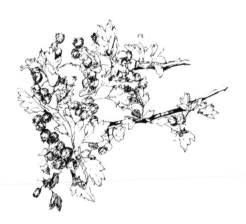

"It's murder!" screamed Roger Barrell, landlord of *The Three Horseshoes*. As the next of kin, he had been requested to formerly identify Old Tom's body. Now he was standing in the kitchen of the dead man's old fashioned cottage. Local builder, Hugh Storey, who had discovered the corpse, remained pale and nervous from the shock.

Less than half an hour before — at about half past eight — Storey had been walking his black labrador bitch along the track towards Markham Wood. As he ambled beside the fields that Tom farmed in his traditional — if muddled manner — he had approached the old man's antiquated Fordson tractor and Massey Harris 'seed drill' backed up to the seed-corn trailer on the headland. Reaching the stationary machinery, the bright September moon lit up the sacks of seed corn on the trailer.

Then the builder has seen something else. There, slumped against the 'drill', was Old Tom. His face was twisted in a hideous contortion of pain. His neck and body were a mass of blood, puckered skin and shattered bone where the lethal pellets from the shotgun's blast had torn him open.

. . . antiquated Fordson tractor and Massey Harris seed drill . . .

"That bastard Younger!" snapped Barrell. "It MUST have been him. Shooting rabbits at night. That's how it happened."

For the second time in less than five minutes, the publican accused Bob Younger, the neighbouring tenant farmer and an impetuous thirty year old bachelor of his uncle's death.

The 'accident' he argued hotly, had occurred just behind a low hedge where the two farms joined. Much more to the point he continued, Younger was notorious for his night-time rabbit shooting. But what proved the case, he declared, was that both Constable Brown, Hugh Storey and himself, had all heard a shotgun being repeatedly fired on Younger's fields that very evening.

Only Joshua Cartwright seemed unconvinced. The retired farmworker with the mass of silver hair had been Tom's best mate since they had made their first catapult together beneath the ash trees of the village school, over sixty-five years before.

But Cartwright was more involved than that. His wife was an intimate friend of Bob Younger's mother, and he in fact, had been a nominal uncle to the boy throughout his life. After Dick Younger had suddenly died in middle age and Bob took on the tenancy of Blackthorn Farm, old Joshua had been like a second father to the lad.

Standing beneath the low beams, Cartwright frowned with confusion and disbelief.

'Hold on,' he seemed to be thinking. 'There's something wrong. It can't be as straightforward as that.'

The point was, he knew Younger too well. And for all the lad's impetuosity, he was certain that Bob would never have left Tom slumped over the seed drill without attempting to help him.

"You don't look convinced," sneered Barrell, "that the crazy boy IS responsible".

"I — I don't know."

"I'm sorry, Joshua," put in Storey, "but it looks pretty obvious to me."

"We shall have a statement soon enough," said Constable Brown. "Just as soon as Younger's been interviewed at Blackthorn Farm".

At that moment the policeman's car radio sounded. It took only seconds to answer. Yet he returned with slow steps. His face was stricken and pale.

"I am sorry Joshua," he murmured, looking directly at Cartwright.

"What's happened?"

"The detective wasn't able to interview Younger," continued Brown trying to lessen the impact of his information.

"Why not?"

"I am afraid that when they reached Blackthorn Farm they came across an unpleasant sight . . . A very unpleasant sight . . . It was Bob Younger." The constable paused for one moment before adding with a dull finality. " . . . He has shot himself."

Momentarily the room around Cartwright seemed to sway; the ceilings and walls dissolved into flux. He noticed Barrell's vindictive look. "That settles it," someone was saying. "Stupid bastard," Barrell was repeating.

But something was not right. Some unspecific doubt kept tugging at Cartwright's mind. Around him the others were preparing to leave. Gradually the room stopped swaying; he glanced at the table and the draining board; at the old clock on the mantelpiece and out through the window at the brilliant full moon. At the table and the window and the brilliant full moon.

"It's a lovely moon tonight," he muttered absently. Storey started.

"That's why I was able to see the body," he said.

"Where he had been loading up the drill with seed corn," mumbled Cartwright. " . . . with seed corn . . . in paper sacks . . ."

Barrell and Storey ignored the old man. Only on Lesley Brown's face was there a puzzled, enquiring expression.

"And — er — by the way," continued Cartwright. "What is this 'ere thing?"

He pointed with his thick finger to the kitchen table where an ancient object lay beside a tin of dog food.

"It's called a PENKNIFE!" spat Barrell.

"Tom made a whistle with that when we boys were in the church choir," mused Cartwright significantly. This time however, Constable Brown, whose own father had a Norfolk smallholding, gave Cartwright a comprehending nod.

'There's too much that doesn't make sense,' thought Cartwright, much later that evening. 'Oh yes, things seemed very convenient. Too convenient. Yet other things didn't add up.

'Why was Tom's penknife in the kitchen? And why hadn't Bob Younger made contact with him or left a message before 'committing suicide'?'

Despite his better nature, Cartwright began to consider who else might benefit from Old Tom or Bob Younger's death. To his surprise there were several suspects.

Involuntarily he couldn't help mistrusting Roger Barrell. Everyone knew that uncle and nephew — Old Tom and Barrell himself — had never remotely seen eye to eye. Moreover, it was common knowledge that Barrell had wanted to sell the old fashioned smallholding and realise the capital while land prices were buoyant. But Old Tom was stubborn and inflexible. He had spent his entire working life on those few fields and meadows. He might well be approaching his seventy fifth birthday, he continually explained, but Elm Tree Farm meant everything to him and farming it was how he intended to die.

The memory of that oft-repeated intention sent an icy shiver through Cartwright. For it was an expression that Old Tom had frequently repeated to builder Hugh Storey. More to the point, Storey had outline planning permission for 25 houses on a meadow at the back of the village. But the scheme was dependent on Storey providing a feasible vehicular access. The intermediatory eighty yards or so was owned by Old Tom. For months on end, Storey had cajoled and tempted him with offers of thousands upon thousands of pounds for that crucial strip. The indifferent countryman had only shrugged with a vague disdain. Money wasn't everything, he pointed out. Besides, not everyone wanted to have dozens of new houses foistered on the village. Moreover, that strip of meadow was where the village boys had always played their games of football. In fact, once, before the war, he had scored a hat-trick there himself. And anyway, he always concluded, he still liked to wander down there on a Sunday morning and meet his old mates as they cheered on their grandsons. To tell the truth, it was one of the high points of his otherwise solitary life.

And so Storey had bitten his lip, not certain if Tom was genuinely sincere in his simple views, or whether he was shrewdly bluffing to raise the stakes even higher.

Another who would benefit, thought Cartwright sombrely, was Sir Paul Henderson, the village's principal landowner and city businessman. He had inherited the estate which was centred around his ivy clad Georgian residence of Upper Hall some years before. Approaching his late thirties he was somewhat overweight but still conveyed a debonair appearance wearing silk cravats, family signet rings and an abundance of aftershave.

Despite his baronetcy and Etonian education, he had never made his mark upon the world. Lacking tenacity, the several imaginative ventures upon which he had embarked had tended, one by one, to fail and fade away. There was something slightly juvenile about his personality and although no-one could properly put their finger on it, there was an unconvincing shallowness in his make-up.

It was reckoned however, that he had done rather well to inveigle a Chelsea fashion designer to be his wife. She was beautiful; sophisticated; and blonde. They had been married nine years and had two children.

How Sir Paul continued to balance his books was a recurring topic of parochial speculation. Rents from the estate of which

The Blackthorns was the largest farm, provided a sizeable income, but outgoings which ranged from inheritance tax to seemingly permanent repair work on Upper Hall, rapidly reduced the balance. When Bob Younger's father had died at the age of 53, Sir Paul had unashamedly held high hopes of repossessing The Blackthorns and selling it off at vacant possession price. To his undisguised chagrin however, the law of land tenure was changed during the subsequent six months and Bob was able to claim succession of tenancy. At a stroke, the value of Blackthorn Farm on the open market was halved. Bob Younger paid his rent; but Sir Paul was not able to realise his capital asset.

Regretfully, mused Cartwright, as he paced his kitchen long after midnight, Sir Paul was not alone in resenting the boisterous and brash young farmer that Bob had become. Niel Bookley, the village schoolmaster, had particularly good reason. His wife Mary, had been a teenage sweetheart of Bob's. After a couple of years however, they had gone their separate ways and Mary had met Niel at Teachers Training College. Bookley had changed a good deal in the intervening years. The adventurous free-thinking radical of student days had settled into a politically aspiring, socially ambitious local figure. Mary had found it impossible to share his new objectives or to find any happiness in accompanying him each weekend to a string of worthwhile but moribund conferences. Mary had never changed. Her greatest relaxation was still to help behind the bar of *The Three Horseshoes*. Her most attentive customer was a local tenant farmer. His name was Bob Younger.

Nobody, with the exception of Mary and Bob, actually knew the truth about their bantering friendship. Quite possibly they didn't even know themselves. But there was gossip. And the gossip had begun to damage Bookley's carefully nurtured public image.

The final character of whom Cartwright thought, was Bob's closest neighbour, photographer, Marcus Pryke. Over the past three years, the pair had engaged in a series of stormy altercations concerning bird scarers on rape fields, gardens being damaged by spray drift, smuts from straw burning; smells from pig muck, flail hedge cutting, mud on the road and cultivating across footpaths. Pryke, who saw himself as the champion of Everymans Rights in the heart of the countryside, had not been overly diplomatic, or even correctly informed in the details of his first complaints to Younger. In turn, the latter — who wasn't one to apologise to anyone, — now gave the big headed impression that whenever there was an anti-social operation that he could still legitimately perform, — such as tractor driving early on Sunday morning, or spreading pig muck on one of his fields — then by a strange coincidence, it would always occur just behind Pryke's cottage.

The latter claimed to work largely from home. But a majority of the locals — being less gullible than they pretended — questioned if the 'work' wasn't of an apocryphal nature. Meanwhile however, the 'photographer' had tastefully converted his timbered cottage into an open-plan studio which was adorned with 'objects d'art'. He drank black coffee; wore an open-necked shirt, a gold bracelet and wooden clogs. An 'impressionistic' photograph of his two children hung over his all-glass desk. Somewhere in Bournemouth, an ex-wife was being supported by his alimony.

Apart from his dealings with Younger, he was a man of popular charm. He affected a considerable knowledge of ski resorts, exclusive art galleries and obscure vineyards in Southern France. His was the sincerity of the efficient survivor.

*　　*　　*

Despite Cartwright's reservations it was still a case of 'fait accompli'. The two inquests revealed nothing that did not tally with the assumed events of the night. And although a police statement emphasised that the death of Younger only 'appeared' to be suicide, the national press soon overlooked the crucial word. One tabloid immediately produced a brazen, double-paged feature on "THE CASE OF THE RABBIT SHOOTING", ... and the rest of Fleet Street soon followed suit. Meanwhile M.P.'s were petitioned to ban late night shooting whilst Markham 'Young Farmer's Club' donated a Guide Dog for the Blind in memory of Bob Younger's name. By and large however, everyone else meekly accepted the first conjecture — of an accidental shooting and an ensuing suicide. Inevitably also, the local police force, already weighed down with other work, came to consider that the case was closed. After all, there was nothing — and nobody — to dispute the evidence.

Except for Joshua Cartwright.

He alone was not convinced. Time and again he reworked the reactions of those involved; And refused to believe that Bob Younger would have committed suicide without attempting to help Old Tom . . . or without leaving a note or a message.

For over a month that autumn, he was to be seen restlessly pacing the village, mumbling to himself about 'the full moon on the night of the murder' and 'the penknife on the table at Old Tom's cottage'.

His investigation had begun in that tragic last week of September. It was when the hawthorn berries were resonant and rosy in Blackthorn Lane. It had continued as the gorgeous red fruit of the guelder rose and the glossy purples of the elderberry bushes became a mass of imperial colour in the meadow next to Old Tom's farmyard. Ignoring the strange looks and the innuendoes and the callous remarks which were made of his eccentric obsession, he persevered as the dock seeds and the dogwood went a velvety red. Unabashed and undaunted, he searched and he probed as a gentle first frost turned the hedgerow maples into a glorious profusion of syrupy gold. And he doggedly battled on, as the spindle seeds glowed orange, as the travellers joy turned silver and the larch in the garden at Blackthorn Farm, became a regal and flaring yellow.

Then there was a bitter frost. Suddenly it was minus six degrees centigrade. The leaves fell off the Ash trees and the branches lay bare as if attacked by hooligans overnight. It was November the third. It was also the night of the Parish Council meeting.

*   *   *

Everyone of Cartwright's suspects attended. Sir Paul Henderson was in the chair. The other council members were landlord Roger Barrell, builder Hugh Storey, teacher Niel Bookley, photographer Marcus Pryke, P.C. Lesley Brown and Joshua Cartwright. Amongst the parishioners who listened from the

101

floor was a blunt talking newcomer. Kurt Nixon.

The meeting opened with the Chairman solemnly paying tribute to the two departed parishioners who had so willingly served the village.

Cartwright said nothing; but his eyes were restless and throughout the meeting he was visibly tense and agitated.

The agenda was dealt with point by point. Could the bus shelter be repaired? What about the road sign on the Dudley Corner 'S' bend? Should the cricket club be charged a rent for using the village hall as their pavilion? Could the parish council write to the County Council and complain that the mobile library always called at dinner time?

Finally, they came to item number six:

"Is there any other business?" asked Sir Paul, with brusque efficiency. "If not, I would like to . . . "

"Yes" interrupted Cartwright. "The deaths of Old Tom and Bob Younger".

The others glanced at him impatiently.

"We have already covered that sad occurrence once tonight," remarked the Chairman.

"Here, here," said Hugh Storey.

"The only thing," persisted Cartwright, "is that we had a minutes silence for Old Tom. The chairman said that he had been killed in an accident."

"That's right. That was what the police established," replied Sir Paul, with upper-class assurance.

"But he wasn't killed in an accident," answered Cartwright slowly. There was a dogged and determined certainty in his voice. The village hall fell silent; The ticking of the large old-fashioned clock seemed louder.

Finally Barrell spoke. There was an edge of malice to his question.

"How did he die then?"

Sir Paul was about to say something about addressing the chair, or of the matter being beyond the scope of the meeting but Cartwright had already begun.

"No," he said, with a voice of taut emotion. "Tom wasn't killed in a shooting accident." Again he paused and his brow puckered and his rugged chin sagged. "Tom," he began bitterly, "was . . . was . . . murdered!"

102

A murmur of scepticism followed the farmworker's statement.

"What proof have you got?" asked Niel Bookley.

"My proof," said Cartwright slowly, "is that Bob Younger... Oh God ... was also murdured." He paused. Then whispered hoarsely, "The murderer is here tonight."

The room erupted. Amidst the uproar Sir Paul was quietly asked by Constable Brown if he would allow Cartwright to continue. In fact, it was the policeman who brought the meeting to order.

"These are very serious accusations," observed Sir Paul loudly, "And I have no doubt that they fall completely outside the parameters of this meeting. However, as Little Markham is such a small community it may be better ... "

"Mr. Chairman," cut in Niel Bookley. "Could Joshua explain how he 'knows' that Tom was murdered?"

"Because of the penknife," replied Cartwright.

"What on earth has that got to do with it?" asked Marcus Pryke.

Cartwright shot him a quick glance. "Because Tom was meant to be drilling. At the time of the murder, he was supposed to be opening seed-corn bags. Don't you understand. It's impossible. The damn things are stitched up like chastity belts. Tom would *never* have gone drilling without a penknife. There isn't a farmworker in Europe who would go drilling without something to cut open the bags with."

"But there might have been a knife or something on the drill," countered Roger Barrell.

"Yes! There *might* have been. But there wasn't! Don't you see. Someone lured Tom away from his house. They probably played on his kind old nature by asking him for help. But when they reached the drill he was ... " Cartwright's voice faltered ... "you know the rest ... shot in cold blood."

"It could still have been Bob Younger," said Sir Paul. "Old Tom might have forgotten his penknife."

"But he didn't. And it wasn't Bob Younger."

"How can you be so sure?" questioned Hugh Storey.

"Because of the moon. It was a FULL moon. All his life Bob Younger had been going out shooting rabbits at night. And one of the first things you learn is that the rabbits are ten times as nervous on a moonlit night as they are when it is windy and pitch black. *Those* are the best conditions for that job. No. Bob would never have gone out rabbit shooting on the night in question."

"So what is *your* version of events then?" asked Sir Paul.

"That someone wanted to kill either Old Tom or Bob Younger. But they had to be clever. They couldn't simply murder someone and then benefit too obviously. So we are faced with two choices.

Let's say that the murderer wanted to kill Old Tom. Now, if they could make it appear that he had been 'accidentally shot', they then had a perfect murder. Except, that to prevent Younger denying the 'accident', they had to subsequently fake his 'suicide'.

Alternatively, if the real target was Younger, they first had to murder Tom, so that Bob had a sufficiently strong reason to 'commit suicide'."

"Ingenious," observed Bookley thoughtfully.

"And far fetched," muttered Storey.

"Too much T.V." said Pryke.

There was a silence. The old farmworker seemed lost for words. As if subdued into silence by the horrifying indifference of those around him.

"Can we go now?" asked Barrell lazily. The tide was turning. The incredulity had resurfaced. The flippancy returned. There was a shuffling of papers and a moving of chairs.

"No," cut in a hard voice. It was Nixon. He slapped down an identity card. It read: . . . 'Detective Sergeant'

"I've got to admit," he declared in a brutal tone, "that it was a long while before I took Joshua seriously. I've got to confess," he continued in his raw, East-End vernacular, "that I thought he was cuckoo as well. But he's proved his point."

The room fell silent.

"Yesterday I re-opened the case."

"So we are all 'real' suspects," remarked Sir Paul softly.

"You all have a motive," replied Nixon. "But that is the difference. Between 'motive' and actually committing two such violent and calculated murders."

"What *I'm* looking for, is someone with powers of manic self interest. Someone totally and utterly without scruple. Someone who has murdered twice. Someone who won't hesitate to murder again."

"Surely though," said Storey nervously, "some of us have got alibis."

"Unfortunately not," answered Nixon. "According to the pathologist's report, the deaths occurred between half-past seven and a quarter-past eight. It's astonishing! None of the main suspects has an alibi for those forty five minutes."

The room was very still.

"Niel Bookley," continued the detective, "claims to have been marking the third form's history project but his wife was working at *The Three Horseshoes* and can't vouch for him. Roger Barrell wasn't seen in the *Horseshoes* because he felt tired and was allegedly resting upstairs before the evening rush. Hugh Storey was quietly doing his monthly V.A.T. in the portacabin office of his builders yard. Sir Paul was watching television but his wife and children were in London and he received no visitors. The only person with an alibi is Marcus Pryke. He was photographing a conservation seminar in Scotland. A shot that he took of the event on the same evening as the murder appeared on the front cover of October's *'County and Shire'* magazine."

Carefully removing a glossy publication from a brown paper bag, the policeman quietly passed it around the table. On the inside page an italic caption explained, *"Our front cover shows well-known celebrity and president of the Rural Landscape Society, James Orlando, weeding a sapling at a Conservation Day held at Loch Nev Castle on September 24th."* The photograph itself portrayed Orlando, with weeding hook in hand, clearing nettles and grass from a young oak tree in early evening.

"Sunset," added Constable Brown, "occurs at about seven o'clock during the fourth week of September."

"Which bring us back," resumed Nixon, "to a killer." He looked around the table with a wearisome grimmance. "An exceptionally detached thinker. Someone who might not expect to reap any benefits from his sordid investment for at least five years." He paused and looked sadly at Sir Paul.

"The trouble, Sir," he began, "is that once I had accepted Cartwright's evidence, I had to try and think as ruthlessly as the murderer. I know how much Bob Younger's death would improve your financial standing. But quite honestly," he concluded with an almost apologetic air, "I don't think that you have really got it inside you."

"Then I came to Niel Bookley, the deceived husband who had married the wrong girl; the man with the limitless ambitions. The back street boy who had fought himself up in the world. Oh yes, Niel had the ruthless streak. Ruthless enough to get out of his poverty stricken slum. Ruthless enough to expose Cruikshank's little fiddle with the school's transport money so that the friendly old buffer was 'relieved of his duties', whilst you, Niel Bookley, were promoted to be England's youngest headmaster. The problem is, that there was nothing in it for you. Men like you don't cry and shoot people when their wives leave them. They ignore them. They just move on, ruin somebody else's marriage and turn up with someone twice as attractive again. I'm sorry," surmised Nixon, "but I just don't think you actually loved Mary, or for that matter anyone else enough to commit a murder."

Brookley sat grim faced, his lips tight and his cheeks drawn. Then he glowered at Cartwright as if to say, 'You're the one that has told the police all about my private problems. Poking your nose into other people's business!'

"As for Hugh Storey," resumed Nixon, "Well yes, he also had a motive. The usual one: Money. But Hugh Storey had a problem as well. I'm sorry, Hugh, but you are too much of a work-horse to ever murder. I won't say that you are actually too dull, but you're certainly too uninspired. Look at you. All your life you've been a builder. And yet you've never once designed a single wall that wasn't already on the architect's drawing. No, you could never have devised such an elaborate and complicated plan."

"Then I expect I could," interrupted Barrell with a querulous hardness in his voice. "Senile bastard!" he stabbed at Cartwright.

The room was thick with tension. No love had ever been lost between those two men. Theirs was the difference of two philosophies. One the dependable, self deprecating countryman; the other, flashy, gregarious and over talkative.

"No Barrell," cut in Nixon, "You are a boozy, big-mouthed boy in man's clothing, but I am looking for someone of *real* calibre." He paused, and then his voice was bitter and vindictive. "Someone who could execute two murders; someone who could plan five years ahead; someone who likes the good life but can't afford it. Someone who would rather murder and marry someone else's money than apply himself to proper work." Nixon swung round and glared at Pryke before continuing, "and someone — in fact the only person here — who was so certain of his guilt that he had to fake an alibi. But you got it wrong!"

"You're being absurd!" exclaimed Pryke. "The photograph in 'County and Shire' proves it. You could find yourself in court on a charge of slander for this. The old man's addled your brain."

"No!" retorted Cartwright, producing the magazine for the others to scrutinize again.

"Our front cover shows . . . James Orlando . . ."

"It took me a while," said Nixon, "to understand Joshua's point, and I do agree that you went to Loch Nev and took a photograph. But the snap of James Orlando actually weeding a tree — well that was one you took earlier in the day, *and then superimposed* in the foreground of the photograph of Lock Nev church."

"I have warned you about slander!" snapped Pryke.

"I am sorry," interrupted Sir Paul, "but I simply cannot follow Joshua's theory that it is a composite photograph. As far as I can see it's a perfectly normal record of an out-door conservation meeting."

107

"Absolutely."

"But it's *not!*" retorted Cartwright. "Just tell me," he pleaded, "just tell me, which way does a church point?"

"Well – er – Easterly, I think,"

"And from where do the British Isles receive their prevailing wind?"

"The South West," answered the Chairman, not a bit enlightened.

"And on which side of the tree that James Orlando was weeding, is the stake which supports the sappling from the prevailing wind?"

"Er – the church side – the er – easterly side."

"Yes," sliced Cartwright's voice. "The easterly side. And that is the major clue. Because when I first saw it, I thought to myself, 'but that can't be right'. Because Lock Nev is in Scotland. And it's a terribly wind-swept place. No decent countryman would *ever* put a tree stake on the 'other side' of the prevailing wind, because the rubber tie wouldn't prevent it from growing on an angle. So Constable Brown made enquiries at the Loch Nev station. Every stake is to the *west of the trees!*"

"The point is," cut in Nixon. "Pryke wasn't there in the afternoon. He was journeying back to Markham. He knew that he could provide his alibi for he had a photograph of the church, taken the evening before, and scores of snaps of Orlando doing his celebrity stunt of 'maintaining a tree'. But he made one mistake. When he superimposed the snap upon the background, he got it *back to front!* The stake was on the eastern, or church, side of the tree."

"So why," continued Nixon, "did you go to such elaborate lengths to produce an alibi if you had nothing to fear? Why didn't you print one of the hundred other shots you had taken during the morning session? Wouldn't those looking over the Loch have been just as attractive. I'll tell you why. Because they wouldn't have proved you were still in Scotland on the evening of the murder!"

Until that moment the photographer had successfully controlled himself. But now his face was taut with rage; his body tensed forward. Then he was moving. His chair crashed onto the floor. In two strides he reached the rickety door; in a single movement it was opened and he was leaping through and out to his waiting car. Where he was siezed by the waiting police.

"Photographer!" spat Cartwright with disgust.

"But I don't quite understand." began Sir Paul.

"He had the least motivation of anyone. Unless . . . "

Cartwright gave the baronet a sympathetic nod. Sir Paul may not have noticed the special look which his wife had developed for Pryke at the village fête or the Christmas social. He may have missed the strands of blonde hair that Nixon had carefully picked from the photographer's pullover; and he may have attached no significance to the accidental meetings of man and beautiful woman in the woods on morning walks.

But others percieved the truth.

It was the hard and callous truth that when Marcus Pryke, confidence trickster extraordinaire, had calculatingly seduced Lady Suzanne Henderson into a romantic liaison, and then compromised her into marriage, he had every intention that her ex-husband's settlement would include Blackthorn Farm at its full freehold and tenant free market price.

Pryke would have never needed to work again.

And why?

* * *

Because for generations past, the men of Little Markham had invested all of their skill and their strength into the ploughing and the sowing; into the haytime and the harvests of Blackthorn Farm. They had been badly paid and poorly housed. They had been hungry, rainsoaked and chilled to the bone. But one family, one family in particular, had become synonymous with the place. It is they who had been the shepherds and the stockmen, the horsemen and the harvest reapers. They were renown as independent and 'Chapelite' people. They had learned the Scriptures off by heart and abided by every one of the Ten Commandments.

Now from that vast family of farmworkers, there is only one remaining silver-haired descendant.

It should not be too difficult to deduce his name.

Also by Ashley Cooper

The Long Furrow

Three thousand years of rural history from the Suffolk-Essex border telling the story of the land and those who worked it from the last ice age to contemporary times. Complete with the memories of over seventy local people including the horsemen, shepherds, drovers, blacksmiths and threshing contractors of the bygone era, the book also includes chapters on Roman Gestingthorpe; Arthur Young; the farmworkers' strike of 1893; Harvest time and horkeys; the Tithe War; the Great Depression and a special section devoted to wildlife, and a local ecological survey.

The Long Furrow is Ashley Cooper's first book and was largely quoted in *The Reaper's Year*, a play written and performed by the Eastern Angles Touring Theatre Company.

Fifth print now available. ISBN 0 900227-82-6

"I've enjoyed *The Long Furrow* immensely, in fact it's just the sort of book I wish I had written myself."
David Richardson
Presenter of Anglia Television's 'Farming Diary'

"...Ashley Cooper in his excellent book *The Long Furrow*."
Quentin Seddon
Author of 'The Silent Revolution', BBC Books

The Khyber Connection
The Furrow and the Raj

Returning home from a rucksack expedition around India at the age of 23, Ashley Cooper was intrigued to discover that a neighbouring farmworker had also visited the sub-continent – with the Suffolk Regiment in 1921.

Eventually the author interviewed over 70 local people from the Suffolk-Essex border who had also served in India. Privates from the local regiments, Gurkha officers, retired tea planters and their wives, all describe their lives.

But the book is not all nostalgia. A complete section is devoted to local men who served in the **BURMA CAMPAIGN** of World War Two and who depict again the heroism of Imphal and Kohima and the jungle camps in which they lived.

Many other surprising connections between India and the Suffolk-Essex area are also unearthed, and by examining local newspapers, the reaction of East Anglians to the Indian Mutiny is investigated.

Finally the reader is taken on a 7000 mile journey from the plains of North India to the coasts of Kerela and from the snow packed Himalayas to the rugged boulders of The Khyber Pass as India is explored again.

ISBN 0-900227-81-8

"Fantastic. I'm thrilled that at last someone has recorded what the average soldier went through during the Burma Campaign. I've also had some good laughs as well. It's definitely written in a style of its own. Superb!"

Douglas Legg
Retired Sudbury Printer. Stationed in India 1942-45

"...an original and highly successful attempt to examine the impact of India on one small area of England. ... Cooper's book is one that merits the admiration of anyone remotely interested in India and is a work to be noted by historians amateur and academic..."

Chowkidar (Vol. 4 No. 6)
The magazine of the British Association for Cemeteries in South Asia

JUST PUBLISHED

Heart of Our History

Five hundred years of **VILLAGE LIFE** along the Suffolk-Essex border, including the memories of 90 local people and numerous excerpts from historic manuscripts.

Beginning with the era when parishes were largely self-governing – with their overseers, perambulations, surveyors and constables, the book continues with human memories. Of 'Dad's Army', village cricket, public houses, being 'in service', the cottage economy, the coming of education and 'how' people lived in the last years before electricity and the motor car transformed daily life in the Sudbury-Halstead-Hadleigh area.

ISBN 0-9524778-0-7

ASHLEY COOPER farms on the Suffolk-Essex border where he was born in 1952.

His first book, *The Long Furrow* was published in 1982 and has since been reprinted four times. He is particularly interested in recording human memories and has subsequently written *The Khyber Connection* whilst continuing to research a sequel to *The Long Furrow*.

Tales of Woodland and Harvest is his first work of fiction.

Elizabeth Martland spent her childhood years in Sudbury, Suffolk where the surrounding area inspired a love of countryside and floral subjects. She is currently completing a degree course in Illustration and Graphic Design at Brighton Polytechnic.